The Adventures of Dick Ryder:
Four Play Volume 2 (4 Stories)

by

Candy Nytes

PUBLISHED BY:
Lemon Tree Publishing
Copyright © 2012 Candy Nytes
CandyNytes.com

This is a work of fiction. All characters, names, places and events are the product of the author's imagination or used fictitiously.

Editing: Dragonfly Editing

ISBN-13: 9781927623114

Table of Contents

SWING TIME

It was a Sunday morning. I was lazing in my bed reading the morning newspaper. I was catching up on the entertainment news. I looked over at my clock. It was just after eleven am. I was getting hungry and figured I should head down to the kitchen to make myself some toast and coffee.

It was around that time when folks were either in church or coming home from church. I forget if church usually starts at ten or eleven. Maybe it depends on the denomination. I had given up on church a long time ago. You understand. My folks died when I was young. That kinda shook my faith in anything that couldn't be touched or seen.

I folded the newspaper and tossed it on my guest's side of the bed. There was nobody there. I had slept alone last night. Had slept alone the last few nights. I wasn't sad about it. I was doing some reflecting and thinking. Janet had practically ignored me now for about a week. Maybe longer. I was trying not to think about it. She had a way of getting under my skin. Half of me liked that. The other half, um, not so much.

I got out of bed wearing my blue satin pajama bottoms. Did I tell you how much I like blue? Probably. I walked downstairs into the kitchen and pulled some twelve grain bread out of the freezer. I didn't actually count. That's what it said on the package. Could've been false advertising, but still, it made me feel healthy. I popped two slices into the toaster and set it for dark.

I made myself some fresh brewed coffee, from one of those fancy coffee machines that grinds the beans for you fresh. Mine was a Capresso. If you've never had a coffee machine with grinder before, you're missing out. Really. It tastes a lot better than even coffee ground as recently as the day before.

I was looking out my kitchen window, holding a butter knife in my hand. I don't use it for butter, but that sounds better than margarine knife. Anyway, I was waiting for the toast to pop. I was watching a hummingbird have a feast on the feeder I had put out in the backyard for them. Gorgeous creatures.

The doorbell rang. Maybe the Jehovah's had missed me at service this morning and were coming by to check up on me. Or it could be a delivery. But a ringing doorbell on a Sunday morning. Okay, it was almost afternoon. Still, a ringing doorbell is not normally from friends or close acquaintances. They're liable to knock.

Nevertheless, I was curious. I went to see how it was. Maybe I should've put a shirt on, but I was halfway decent anyway. I peeked into the peephole. Dammit if it wasn't Janet. I swallowed. My heart thumped a little harder than it should've.

I opened up the door. Smiled my biggest smile. She held her hands in front of her. She was wearing a salmon colored dress with shoulder straps. She looked like a dish.

"Hello Janet," I said.

"Hi Dick."

We stood there like that for a long pause. She glanced down at the ground. Then she looked back up at me and stroked her index down my abs. Her nail scratching ever so softly, tickling me. I started to feel aroused.

"Can I come in?"

I swallowed. I coughed.

"Uh, yeah, sure, come on in."

I opened the door wider to let her in. My cock was starting to bulge and grow firm in my pajama pants. It would soon be a flag pole pointing where it shouldn't.

I barely closed the door when Janet put her arms around me and kissed me passionately on the lips. I was hard now. Like a steel pole. My cock pushed against her upper thigh. We kissed for a long time. I heard a buzzer go off in the kitchen. Shit, that was my toast, probably burning by now.

I disengaged from her embrace.

"Shoot," I said, "I think that's my toast. It's burning, let me go get it quick. I ran off into the kitchen. My cock was banging around in my pants like a dog's panting tongue.

Janet came in after me to see what the fuss was about. Smoke snaked from the toaster. The coffee machine started to snort and splutter. Coffee was almost ready. Thank God for small mercies. At least I could have some coffee. I flicked up the toaster lever. Two charcoal bricks popped up out of the toaster. Well, not fully charcoal, but burnt beyond edible.

Janet snickered cutely. She came up behind me and put her arms around me. She moved them down around my stomach. I swallowed hard. It had been too long since we had been intimate. Her touch was thrilling. Ticklish and titillating. She pushed her hands slowly under my waist band and down towards my groin. She caressed my pubic hair and moved her hands apart and down towards my thighs.

My cock was straining hard to get out of my pants. She took her hands and with her fingernails she caressed the sides of my balls. I quivered and my knees almost buckled. I wanted to turn around and grab her. Throw her over the side of the kitchen table and just fuck her right there. Hard and fast. But this feeling was too great. Too intense. I wanted to see what she would do. This was one of the first times she was taking control of our sexual intimacy without any input or mind control from me. I loved it. It was all natural. All her own doing without me having to use my super power to unleash her sexual animal.

I braced myself against the kitchen counter, gripping the sides of it. I breathed deeply. Janet moved her hands down my thighs again and then slowly and carefully she brought her fingertips inside my thighs and scratched at my balls with her fingernails, gently and just around the edges. I wanted to grab her hands and have her jerk me off. My cock was swollen, hard and aching.

She pulled her hands out of my pajama pants and then pushed them down to my ankles. She turned me around and kissed me deeply on the mouth. She grabbed at the base of my throbbing penis with her right hand and pulled on it gently. I felt a dribble of cum exit my head. She tugged on me again, and then again.

She pulled away from me and looked down at my erect dick. She bit her lower lip.

"Ooh," she said, "somebody is happy to see me."

She tugged on him again and then knelt down on her knees. She looked at the cum leaking from the tip of my cock and flicked her tongue over it and licked at my head. I exhaled loudly. Sighing. She looked up at me and smiled.

"What?" she asked.

I looked down at her with my hard, large cock in her hand pointing at her mouth.

"You're going to get into trouble if you keep that up missy," I said, trying to sound as stern as I could.

She pinched her mouth into an o.

"Who, me?"

I nodded. And then I closed my eyes as she started massage my meaty member. Pulling on my shaft and caressing my balls with her left hand. I felt like warm clay in her hands. She was squeezing me and pulling on me like I was a squeeze toy.

I looked down at her. She was looking up at me. She stuck her tongue out but it didn't reach my penis. I thrust my cock at her and she backed away and pulled her tongue back into her mouth. If she was going to play hard to get I was going to play hard to get too. She stuck her tongue out for me again. I really wanted to lay my cock on it and watch my white cum, thick as pudding ejaculate onto that wet pink triangle, but I was going to play hard to get.

I pulled myself away, grinding my butt against the drawer. She pushed her head in towards me, flicking her tongue and I thrust my hips off to the left, my cock just brushed past her tongue, escaping. She pulled back and came at my cock again, I thrust my hips off to the right and she missed me again.

"Bad boy," she said. "Now you're going to get punished."

She grabbed my cock hard in her right hand, steadying it, and then she pulled me into her mouth. Her hot, wet mouth felt like home. She started to suck on down my shaft and then slowly she sucked back up, not quite letting the head of my penis out of her mouth.

I was insane with lust and desire. I grabbed her red hair in two fistfuls in each of my hands and I thrust my cock deep down her throat. He nose squashed into my pubic hair. I pulled out of her mouth, but not all the way. Then I fucked her deep down her throat again. I held her against my pubic hair and counted to ten. Then I pulled her off my cock. She gasped for air as she came off me.

"I told you that you'd get into trouble," I said.

My cock was glistening with her saliva, it was dark pink and stood proud like a soldier. She opened her mouth and I fucked her in the face again and again. On the third deep throat I held her face against my lower stomach for fifteen seconds. I counted slowly. I pulled her off my cock slowly and right at the end she yanked herself off. She gasped for air, deeply. Her eyeshadow was blurry, her eyes had misted involuntarily.

I picked her up. Pulled her dress up to see that she wasn't wearing any panties. I grabbed her in both hands by her ass, scooping her up with her thighs on my forearms, spreading her legs apart. I placed her wet pussy on my cock and I slipped into her tight vagina like a glove. She gasped.

"I haven't had him for a while," she said.

"You're gonna get him now."

I carried her out of the kitchen and up the stairs, bouncing her as I went. She was moaning and panting as we made it into the bedroom. I lay her down on the bed and knelt before her open pussy with my hard cock inside her.

I grabbed her ankles and spread her legs apart as wide as they'd go. I fucked her deeply and I fucked her hard. I worked her up until she was moaning and writhing and telling me to fuck her harder. Then I stopped and pulled my cock out of her.

"Nooo," she said. "Put him back in."

I rubbed my wet cock head against her lips and she writhed and tried to push herself onto me. I pulled away.

"Nooo," she said. "I want him in me."

And I thrust him back in as deep as I'd go, banging up against her cervix. Then I pulled completely out of her.

"Nooo," she said again.

So I thrust my cock back into her, deep and fast. She gasped and sighed. I repeated this several times. Pulling myself out each time until she begged to have my cock back inside of her. I pulled out one last time and waited.

"You know what to do," she said, her breath heavy and her voice hoarse.

"No I don't," I said. "Tell me."

She reached for my cock with her hand but I backed away out of reach.

"I want to hear you say it," I said. "Do you want my cock to fuck you or not?"

"Yes, yes, fuck me with your gorgeous cock."

"That's better."

I thrust inside her and then lay down on top of her, resting on my elbows as I thrust with my hips, fucking her as I watched her face turn even more beautiful as she enjoyed my cock in her pussy. I kissed her mouth. Her lips were plump and full. Her face had a radiant glow and her eyes sparkled. I kissed the scar on the corner of her eye.

I thrust rhythmically and steadily, watching her. I fucked her for several minutes as she stared into my eyes.

"Cum for me," I said, "if you enjoy my cock then cum for me."

And I fucked her harder and deeper and faster. She moaned.

"Oh my god Dick."

I looked into her eyes. She looked off to the side.

"Oh my god, I'm cumming," she said.

I fucked her and as she came I kissed her on her breasts and on her neck and on her mouth. She cried as she came.

I pulled myself out of her, kneeling up on the bed in front of her and she grabbed my cock with her hand and rubbed it up and down as I ejaculated big gobs of cum all over her stomach and breasts. She kept pulling on me and I kept cumming in squirts. One pump of my cum ended up on her lower lip which she licked up with her tongue.

I massaged my cum into her belly and over her breasts.

"It's the best, soothing cream, for blemish free skin," I smiled at her.

She smiled at me, but there seemed a deep sadness in her eyes. She dabbed at her eyes with the corner of the sheet. We climbed under the bed and she cuddled up along my side. She put her hand over my chest and stroked my hair there. She looked up at me and I looked down at her.

"I love you," she said, in the barest whisper. I couldn't be sure if I heard her properly. It might have been the rustling of the sheets.

"I beg your pardon," I said.

She looked up at me and swallowed. Then she looked across my chest at nothing in particular.

"I love you, Dick," she said again.

This time I definitely heard her. I looked up at the ceiling. I thought I could see images in the textured finish of the paint. Sometimes you can find the faces of strange monsters up there. In other words, I didn't know what to say. It felt awkward for a moment. I looked down at her again. I had to say something, but what. I think I might love her, or could love her, but I wasn't ready for that. The first and last time I had told a woman I loved her she had cheated on me. That was my high school sweetheart V.

You might have remembered that story. If not, it's not worth the retelling. Anyway, she broke my heart and I was never going to let that happen again. I wasn't ever going to make myself vulnerable like that again. No sirree. Not me.

And yet, dammit if Janet hadn't kinda burrowed into me somehow. Like a burr, I wasn't sure if the sensation was pleasant or uncomfortable.

"I like you to," I said.

I mean, I had to say something right? I couldn't just leave it hanging like that. I'm not a totally insensitive jerk. Yeah, I like to fuck, and I like to fuck a lot of women, but that doesn't automatically put me in the jerk column.

I mean, this beautiful woman has just bared her soul to me. Okay, she's just bared her heart to me, same diff anyway. I had to say something you know. And I couldn't speak the L word. I mean, I guess I did, at least the l word with the small l, not the big bomb, big letter L word she had dropped on me. Still, that's gotta count for something right?

I looked away just after I'd said it. I felt a little uncomfortable. It suddenly got pretty toasty in my room under these sheets.

"That's okay," she said.

And I know what she meant. She meant it was okay I couldn't tell her I loved her. But I don't think she meant that it was okay that I didn't love her. There's a difference there, I think. Geez, this shit just got a whole lot more complicated and my mind was spinning.

Did I love her? Is that what she was wondering? Fuck, I was wondering that myself. Sure, she made me feel different inside, someplace deep in my chest. I hadn't felt that for almost twenty years. I promised myself I wouldn't feel like that ever again.

But here I was. Starting to feel it. That little bruise in your heart. It feels fragile, right? Like you've just taken a hit, but it's healing and there's a part in the healing where it starts to feel good. But it's vulnerable and you're just about to get hit again, and a whole world of hurt is about to open up inside your heart and kill you. Slowly, you'll bleed to death, lose your will to live.

No thanks, I think I'll stay on this side of the fence. The liking side of the fence. The grass still looks pretty green. But that green grass over on the big L side of the fence. Shit, that's hiding a pit of vipers.

Speaking of vipers. I thought I could see some snakes up in the ceiling on that textured finish. Pretty sure I'll have nightmares of snakes tonight.

Wasn't the snake, the right hand hit man of Eve, that got Adam in that world of hurt back in the bible? Pretty sure it was. See what I'm talking about? Snakes and women, and apples too I suppose, but the snakes and women, they worm into your heart and eat it hole. Then they spit you out, and all you've got left is a rotten core where feelings used to be. Good feelings.

Nay, liking is good. Liking will do just fine for now. Damn, this shit just got a whole lot more complicated than I expected it too.

I got up out of bed. I pulled on some boxer briefs from my drawer. All of sudden I felt sorta vulnerable there, naked.

"Let me get us some coffee," I said, and I walked out the bedroom and went downstairs.

I knew she watched after me. I stood at the counter, smelling the coffee and looking outside. The hummingbird was still there. I watched him and admired him. Didn't know if it was a he or she, but to me it was a he.

He had it right. With his beak he drank from one flower and then the next. At least they looked like flowers on my hummingbird feeder. That's kinda like me. I bed one beautiful woman and then another. It works for the hummingbird in feeding, and it works for me in my feeding, if I can call it that.

Listen, I'm not trying to be crass. But this is how I roll. I think. Hummingbirds don't mate for life. Really, like in the wild. Okay, fine, I know I'm not a hummingbird but I'm trying to deal with this minefield before me. Dare I give way to feelings? You want to know the truth?

I'm scared okay. Yeah, big old Dick Ryder is scared. Scared shitless in fact. Feelings didn't work out well for me last time.

I shook my head and poured two mugs of coffee. I placed them on a tray with the sugar bowl and a small coffee carafe of almond milk. I took it back upstairs. Janet was propped up in bed reading the newspaper. Her breasts were magnificent. Her dark cherry nipples like buttons I wanted to sew onto my mouth. I placed the tray between us and got into the bed next to her.

I took my coffee and drank. Coffee had a way of making me clear the cobwebs from my mind. It tasted good.

"Have some coffee," I said to her.

She took her coffee and put some milk and sugar in it. She sipped it carefully like it was liquid gold.

"I'm glad you decided to come and visit me. I've missed you," I said.

She sipped more coffee and cradled it in her hands. She looked at me.

"I thought it was about time. I wanted to see if you missed me."

"Did you get the wine I left several days ago?"

She nodded.

"It was delicious. We drank it all."

"We did, did we."

"Yes, we did."

Here we go, I thought, starting off with the games. This is why I don't get emotionally involved. This and a whole bunch of thousand other reasons. Call it, one thousand and one reasons love is an emotional blackmailer. Maybe I should write a book about it. That'd make a pretty good title I think.

"Really though, why haven't you been in touch?" I asked her. I was really interested.

"Well," she said, and then she drank more of her coffee.

I waited. I drank some of my coffee. Then I looked off at the paper between us. It was the city section. A councilor was in trouble with a prostitute. Isn't that always the case. His wife was with him. Showing moral support I suppose. Though she didn't look very supportive. Quite severe in fact.

"I don't know Dick. I'm trying to figure out my feelings that I have for you. For us. I needed some space. I just don't know if I want this."

"Want what?"

"Well, this casual relationship. I don't know if I want it, knowing especially that you're with other women all the time."

"So if I promised fidelity. If I promised monogamy, you'd be happy."

She nodded.

"Why is that important to you? I mean, I've never asked it of you."

She sipped coffee again like it was the lube she needed to oil her vocal cords.

"Because I love you Dick. Can't you see that."

She was looking at her coffee. She wasn't looking at me.

"I need my love to mean something. I want to feel special."

"You are special," I said, "and your love does mean something. Just because I can't reciprocate right now doesn't mean that your love is meaningless."

She didn't say anything for a while.

"Why can't you commit Dick. Is it me?"

I looked at her.

"No, it's not you. I've told you before, I don't know if I can ever commit. I like my life. My bachelor life. Sometimes I get lonely, but then I go out and find company. Besides, I had a very bad experience once. You know that. I'm not willing to go through that again."

"I'd never do that to you," she said.

I knew she meant well. And she probably believed she was telling the truth. But things change over time, people change. Maybe not always, and all people, but the risk is too great for me.

"I know you mean well Janet. I just don't know if I fully trust that. I guess I don't know if I fully trust you... Yet."

She took it well. She wasn't getting moody and upset with me. If she was patient. If she bided her time then maybe, just maybe we could figure it out together.

"I know you've never expected me to be faithful, but I have you know."

I looked at her and smiled.

"Yes, I've never expected that."

"Well, I don't think I'm going to be anymore," she said.

The smile fell off my face like badly glued wallpaper.

"Okay," I said.

"Anyway, I was thinking of going to the swing club in town, but you need to go as a couple. So I was wondering. Would you go with me?"

"What's it called?"

Not that it mattered but I thought it was important, and more than anything I was curious.

"The Swing Set."

She looked at me. I felt like I was in a poker tournament and the player with the biggest stack was staring me down. Wondering if I was bluffing.

"Sure," I said, "I'll go with you."

I was bluffing. But I figured what the hell, maybe if she saw that I was okay with her fucking other guys then she'd leave this matter alone, and we could see where things went naturally. Like a river flowing downstream. Maybe we'd end up in the big ocean of love, or perhaps we'd end up in the mudded estuaries of indifference. Either way we'd end up someplace naturally, not forced.

She smiled.

"Good," she said. "Good. It's this Friday night at ten pm."

"Fine," I said, and I nodded. "Pop on by before then and I'll drive us over."

The rest of the time we lay in bed in light conversation. Talking about the weather. Our gardens, and the flowers we were cultivating. She was scheduled for another trip out of town on Monday. Said she'd be gone for a week to meet with vendors. I promised to drive her to the airport. She liked that.

Friday night was only two sleeps away. And those two sleeps weren't very restful for me. At around nine pm Janet knocked on my door. I was dressed in black slacks and a French blue shirt. You know what color my boxer briefs are by now. If you've been paying attention. My socks were the same color, matching my shirt and briefs.

Janet looked lovely, but in a gauche way. She was wearing a red, skintight one piece dress that was strapless. It also only went down about an inch below her bum and I could tell she wasn't wearing any panties. On her feet she had red high heeled stilettos with black straps over the front. Her hair had been pulled tight behind her head into a sort of bun I think they call it. Her lips had lipstick that matched her dress and shoes. She wore black studious looking glasses that made her look like a school teacher.

She handed me a bottle of red wine. It was a 2008 Smoking Loon Syrah or Shiraz. The bottle was half empty.

"Let's have a drink before we go," she said.

"Sure."

I invited her in and went into the kitchen where I poured the remaining wine into two wine glasses. I returned to the living room and handed her a glass. She was sitting on the couch and her dress was so short that I could see her thighs curving against her lower abdomen. If she opened her legs just by a hair, I'd likely get a glimpse of her naked pussy.

"Cheers," I said, and I clinked her glass and sat down next to her.

"To our grand adventure," she offered.

I could tell she was already tipsy. Perhaps she was relying on liquid courage for tonight's entertainment. I didn't say anything. We sat in silence for a while sipping our wine. I got up to turn on the radio. I selected a jazz CD and put it in. It was The Very Best of Cole Porter. The first song was appropriate. Let's Be Buddies. There'd be a whole bunch of buddies tonight. We were all about to become friends with strangers.

"Are you nervous?" she asked me.

"No," I said.

That was the truth. I didn't mind being an exhibitionist. I was in great shape and I had a big cock. Not a big deal for me to show off my talents.

"Oh," she said.

"Are you?" I asked.

"Oh no," she said.

I could tell she was lying. She wasn't a very good liar. That was one of her charming qualities. The conversation for the next forty or so minutes was thin and dry. Much like the wine. Though perhaps I'm being unkind to the wine. At quarter to ten I suggested we leave.

I helped her up. She was steady on her feet considering she'd by now probably had three glasses of wine.

"You look nice," I said. In a trampy sort of way, I wanted to add, but didn't.

"Thank you. So do you my dear Dick."

And she pushed her index finger against my chest and trailed it down sloppily. Her fingernails were red too. Maybe she'd get lucky tonight. She'd probably get lucky tonight. I mean we were going to a fuck club. Let's face it, that's all it is. A place where strangers come to fuck other strangers. Wasn't my preferred type of scene. You might find that hard to believe, but I prefer to have some sort of intimacy or engagement with the women I fuck.

Anyway, Janet would likely get what she wanted. But was it something she'd enjoy, looking back? Time would tell. I was beginning to feel this was a bad idea.

I held the door to my Maserati for her and closed it after she got in.

"What do you think it'll be like?" she asked, as I drove us there.

I shrugged.

"I have no idea," I said. "Probably full of old, fat people."

She giggled and I smiled.

"Or maybe just Greek gods and goddesses."

"I guess we'll find out," she added.

The Swing Set wasn't in the clubby and hip part of town. I wasn't expecting it to be. It was in the industrial part of town. Appropriate, I thought.

I opened the door to let Janet out and as her right leg came out of the car and found the pavement I saw her bald pussy like an exclamation mark. Suddenly, I wanted to close the door and take her back to my place to have her all by myself. But that would be admitting defeat. So instead, I took her hand and helped her out of my car and into the lion's den.

An attractive, middle aged woman met us at the front door. She took any purses and coats that folks wanted to leave behind. She handed us each a form.

"Please read over our rules and sign this form before returning it back to me."

I read over it. There wasn't much to it. Basically, it just outlined the rules of engagement and etiquette. In a nutshell, everything was through consent and both or all parties, in the cases of orgies, needed to consent before you could fuck like rabbits. Additionally, consent could be withdrawn at any time and had to be honored. Blah, blah, blah.

"I've got butterflies," said Janet, as we handed back our forms.

"So this is your first time then?" asked the lady at the counter.

We both nodded, but she was speaking mostly to Janet.

"Don't worry love. You don't have to do anything at all. You can just get a feel for it tonight if that is what you'd prefer. And if you do prefer to get involved, you'll have the pick of the litter."

She winked at Janet.

"But above all else," she said, "only engage with what you feel comfortable doing."

Janet nodded and the lady pointed us down the hall to her left. Other folks were coming in behind us. We passed by a six foot five bodybuilder. He had a stern look on his face and his bulging arms were crossed over his chest. He was likely the bouncer.

Inside was dimly lit, but your eyes adjusted to it after some time. The light was a soft blue and yellow. It made everyone look much better than I'm sure they were in daylight. At one end of the room was the bar. In front of the bar were waist high round tables without chairs with two, three, four and sometimes more people standing around them.

At the far end of the room, opposite the bar, were "rooms". I say that loosely, they were more like beds with lace canopies surrounding them. Some of these rooms were already taken by couples fucking. It appeared as if you could adjust the light over these rooms. Some where brighter than others. The brighter ones were generally empty, though in one of them a woman was taking care of two men and you could see exactly what was going on.

She had one guy's cock in her mouth and she was sucking him slowly. She was on all fours and another guy behind her was fucking her. She kept looking around and she caught my eye. She watched me watching her, and she flicked out her tongue and with her gaze steady on me she licked his cock, watching me. Then she put him all in her mouth, still looking at me. She took him out and blew me a kiss. I smiled at her.

We walked up to an empty table in the middle of the room. It was about half full at the moment, but more people were coming in all the time. Our vantage point was almost perfect. We could see just about everything we wanted in any direction.

I looked at Janet. She was staring at a table a couple of tables away from us. I followed her gaze. A woman was on her knees holding a cock in each hand. The men were leaning with their backs against the table. They were fully dressed, but she had pulled their hard cocks out from their pants. She was sucking on the one and then she sucked on the other. She took turns rubbing and sucking each cock, oblivious to the conversation the two men were having.

A waitress, dressed appropriately, not scantily, came up to us.

"What are you drinking?" she asked.

Her name tag said "Suze".

I tapped Janet on the shoulder. She was still mesmerized by the woman sucking two hard cocks. She looked at me, and I pointed at the waitress.

"Oh... Uh, just a glass of red wine please," said Janet.

"Scotch on the rocks. The Balvenie if you have it."

"We do," she said, and then she walked off.

I turned back to Janet but she was taken to watching some cocks getting sucked off. The woman, who was naked but wearing a studded collar and matching wristbands saw her watching. She let go of the cock in her right hand and beckoned Janet to her with her finger. Janet looked around and then, when she was sure it was for her she went off to the woman.

"Would you like to suck this cock?" she said to Janet. "It's my husband Mike's."

Mike put out his hand to shake Janet's.

"Pleased to meet you," he said.

Janet smiled at him and shook his hand.

"I'm Linda," said Linda on her knees. She beckoned Janet to kneel down beside her. Janet did so. Linda took Mike's cock in her hand and offered it to Janet. Janet took it in her mouth and started sucking on it. Mike looked down, beaming. I wanted to punch him in the face. But I remembered where I was. My feelings annoyed me. I breathed deeply, regaining my composure.

Mike patted Janet on her head. She looked up at him with his cock still in her mouth. Linda was watching her smiling.

"Try this one," she said to Janet.

She offered the cock she had in her left hand to Janet. They were both average sized cocks, uncircumcised. Janet put it in her mouth and sucked it. You could see the guy practically ready to have an orgasm.

"My turn," Linda said, taking the cock away from Janet and she started sucking on it.

She pulled it out of her mouth.

"Let's see who can get their cock to cum first?" said Linda.

Janet giggled. Linda started sucking her cock rhythmically. Janet took Mike's cock back into her mouth and started to suck it furiously. She pumped him up and down with her fist. She took her mouth away and pumped his shaft with both her hands. Then she went back to sucking it, trying to swallow as much of his meat as she could. If I had a gun I'd probably put red poppies on those two men's chests. I breathed deeply, trying to chill out.

Suze came back with the wine and whiskey. I asked her how much it was. She told me it was twenty bucks. I gave her twenty-five and told her to keep the change.

I took a sip of whiskey, it felt like nectar down my throat. I looked back at Janet. Mike had taken his cock into his own hand and he was pumping his cock eagerly. Linda had stopped sucking her cock to watch. Mike ejaculated his gluey cum all over Janet's face and glasses. She was licking her lips and tasting his essence. When he had finished cumming, she took him into her mouth and sucked him some more.

Then Linda started licking Mike's cum off Janet's face and they started to kiss, deeply, passionately, sharing Mike's cream between them. Mike's friend started jerking himself off, watching these two make out in front of him.

Linda turned to face him and she opened her mouth. He squirted a gout of cum into her mouth, followed by another squirt and another splash. He pointed his cock at Janet and managed to pump a gob of cum onto her lips. Linda licked up the cum off Janet's lips and they kissed passionately, giving each other their tongues. Then Linda pulled away and tilted Janet's face up so she was looking at the ceiling. Janet opened her mouth and Linda dribbled all the cum into Janet's mouth. Janet swallowed and they kissed again. Linda squeezed her cock of one last drip of cum, offering it to Janet who licked it up.

Janet got up and came back to me. She didn't say anything, she took a big gulp of her wine. My whiskey was already finished.

"This is fun," she said.

I didn't say anything. I steamed into my whiskey tumbler, tilted it to my mouth and got a dribble of melted ice-flavored whiskey water.

"Yes, quite," I said.

Across from us a couple of guys without their partners or wives raised their glasses to us. Not to us so much as Janet. I was ready to leave. I'd seen enough, had enough. Janet walked over to them. They introduced themselves as Steve and Roger. Janet took them by the hand and led them past me, looking at me all the time. She took them to a spare room. I turned around and watched them climb under the see-through lace canopy. Steve unzipped her and her dress fell to the floor. She was as naked as a jaybird.

She unzipped Roger's pants and then Steve's. Then she pulled them down as they took off their shirts. They were both a little portly. She grabbed Steve's cock and started to massage it. With her other hand she grabbed Roger's cock and massaged it too. They were already practically erect. She put each one into her mouth tasting them, one at a time. Roger's eye's fluttered. I wanted to punch him in the face too. And Steve.

She got onto the bed on all fours with Roger in front of her. She started sucking his cock like she loved it. Like it was the tastiest lollipop she'd ever had. Steve climbed in behind her, and I watched him put his little prick inside her pussy. She barely felt him, she was too focused on sucking Roger's micro-penis. Okay, maybe I'm being mean, but their cocks were nowhere as big as mine. They weren't looking at me, but I had a pretty good side on view of them.

Somebody tapped me on the shoulder. I turned around and saw two relatively attractive, average sized woman with blonde hair.

"Hi, I'm Sheri," said the one.

"And I'm Margaret," said the other.

"It appears that our husbands have been taken with your wife," said Margaret.

"Perhaps you wouldn't mind our company," said Sheri, winking at me.

"I'd like that very much," I said.

Sheri rubbed my groin.

"Good," she said, we'd like that too.

They led me to a room next to Janet's. It was about ten feet away. We climbed up under the canopy. The light was brighter here. Good, I thought. Janet looked up from sucking Roger's cock. I thought I saw a shadow of disappointment cross her face. I couldn't be sure.

Sheri and Margaret knelt down in front of me and unzipped my pants. They pulled them down with my boxer briefs. I unbuttoned my shirt and took it off.

"Ooh," they both said in unison.

"I've never seen such a huge cock," said Margaret.

She wasn't talking to me, she was talking to her friend Sheri.

"I know," said Sheri smiling, "we've hit the jackpot."

Sheri was holding my cock and offering it to Margaret and then back to herself like it was an ice cream cone. I caught Janet watching, but then she quickly turned away. Roger and Steve had changed places. Now Roger was fucking her from behind and Steve was in front of her. His cock glistening with her pussy juice. She started to suck on it. She started moaning. Mostly for my benefit I figured. Steve and Roger were oblivious to their wives sucking me off.

"Mmm," said Margaret, "I could kneel here sucking this cock all night."

"I know," said Sheri, "but I want to feel this big hunk of meat inside me."

"Your wish is my command," I said.

Sheri and Margaret got themselves undressed. They had ample bosoms and shapely figures. They were neatly trimmed but not bald. Sheri lay down on her back on the bed. Her legs were towards me. I grabbed her behind the knees and spread her legs apart. Her pussy opened up for me and I thrust my cock into it. Margaret climbed on top of her friend, putting her pussy towards Sheri's mouth. She watched me fuck Sheri's pussy and she rubbed Sheri's clit.

Sheri was moaning and Margaret was cooing. I pulled my cock out of Sheri's pussy to see what Margaret would do with it. She grabbed it and rubbed it before holding it steady and sucking on it for a while. Then she guided me back insider her friend. Watching intently as I disappeared inside.

I heard a loud moaning coming from the room next to us. I looked over. Janet was back on her knees and both Roger and Steve were jerking themselves over her. Steve came first. Little spider web squirts of cum over Janet's face. She moaned in encouragement, but it wasn't a real moan. Not like the moaning she did for me.

Just as Steve finished up, Roger came all over Janet's face, she didn't have her glasses on anymore. Roger dribbled a few splashes of cum over her cheeks and onto her mouth. Not much. I could spit more than either of them came. Janet rubbed their cum all over her face and then licked her fingers. Then she sucked on each of them, taking their very last drop. She kept looking at me all this time. I looked away. I had seen enough.

I started fucking Sheri harder. Margaret was rubbing her clit vigorously and Sheri started to quiver.

"Cum Sheri," I said to her, encouraging her, "cum for me."

That's all she needed. She came and I felt her pussy tighten around my cock as she got more slippery and wet. She moaned and groaned. I pulled my cock out of her. Her pussy was wet and swollen and a deep pink. My cock was glistening, almost dripping wet with her pussy juice.

Margaret took it into her mouth and sucked me clean. Then she turned around on all fours and presented her heart shaped ass to me. Her asshole was a brown tight star. I wanted to put my cock inside it, but her pussy was wet and I stuck my finger in her. It was slippery, and warm. My cock pulsated.

Sheri had turned herself around and her head was now under Margaret's pussy and my balls. She grabbed my cock and stuck it in her mouth and sucked it longingly.

"Mmm, I want to taste this later," she said, as she took me out of her mouth and guided me into Margaret's tunnel of love.

Margaret sighed and moaned as I slid all of my cock as deep inside her as it would go. I fucked her hard and fast, grabbing her firmly by the waist. Janet was watching from the table we had been at when we first arrived. She was all alone. She didn't look very happy. I brought Margaret this close to orgasm and then pulled my cock out of her. It was sopping wet from her slippery pussy. Sheri took it in her mouth and suck on it, cooing as she did. She pulled me out and inserted me back into Margaret's eager pussy.

I fucked her hard and fast. She was on the brink of orgasm and I stopped for a while.

"No," she said, "don't. I want to cum."

I started to fuck her again faster and faster. I heard her moaning and groaning and sighing. She was almost sobbing in pleasure. Then I stopped again.

"No, no, please. I need to cum."

And so I gave it to her. I fucked her harder and faster. She took it all. She shook, she sobbed, she groaned.

"Fuuuuuuck!" she exclaimed so loudly that several people looked at us.

"I love this cock," she said, as a wave of orgasm came over her.

I felt my cock burst inside her. I exploded and drenched her pussy in my cum.

"Yes, yes," she said.

I took my cock out. It was dripping with my cum and Margaret's pussy cream. Sheri grabbed it and sucked it deeply. I pulled away from her and got up onto the bed opposite from Margaret. My cock was hard, wet and still throbbing. I was fighting back more cum. Margaret leaned up over Sheri and I saw my cum leak out of her wet pussy into Sheri's hungry mouth. Sheri moaned in pleasure.

Margaret took my cock in her mouth and pumped me with her hand.

"Cum, cum, cum," she said, taking me out of her mouth. And I ejaculated big gobs of cum into her mouth. Filling her with my white vanilla cream. She swallowed.

"Mmm, vanilla cream. You taste so good."

She tried to pump more out of my cock, but I was spent. A drop dribbled from my head which she quickly licked up. She licker her lips. I heard Sheri coo in agreement.

Shortly afterwards Janet and I left. I was satisfied. But the drive home was silent. I dropped her off in front of her house. I didn't walk her to her front door, but I waited until she got in. Not even a thanks for the ride. Her face didn't look so good. Her eyeliner was smudged as was her lipstick. I tried to shake the images of cocks in Janet's mouth out of my head. But I couldn't. It pissed me off. I went to bad mad. Woke up with a heavy cloud over my bed. It was my bad mood.

GOD'S WITNESSES

I was mad. I tossed and turned the whole night. You know that, but it bears repeating. I woke up in a foul mood and lay in bed for a couple of hours longer than I should have. I had sort of lost interest in my business and in my day to day activities.

I puttered around the house idly, not knowing what to do and not really having any direction. I checked in on my business and it was humming along nicely. I was banking money, but it didn't give me any enjoyment like it once had.

I got up early one morning that week and took my coffee out onto the porch. Janet's car was in the driveway across the road. I sat out there sipping coffee as it slowly cooled waiting for her to go to work. I saw her pass by her living room window, which faced the road and me. She didn't see me, I don't think she was looking for me either.

After a bit of time she came out her front door, locked the door behind her and walked down the path to her Mercedes. I waved at her, sitting in my comfy porch chair. She had to have seen me. I mean, she was walking right towards me, looking in my direction until she got to her car. She ignored me. That stung a little bit. I was trying to make a peace offering.

She got into her car, reversed out her driveway and onto the road until she was parallel with me. She looked my way again. Again, I waved. She looked away and drove off. She didn't speed off, or burn rubber, though that might have been more appropriate. No, she just drove off with me in her rearview. Well, not really in her rearview, but that's the expression, right?

Fuck it, I thought to myself. If that's how she wants to be, then that's how it'll be. I cut off the small piece of my bruised heart and fed it to the hungry dogs of ambivalence. She wasn't going to get her claws into me like she had, again.

I was a free agent. I was going to have some fun. Take my mind off things with some other woman or women. I started to get that giddy feeling in my stomach I hadn't had for a while. It felt good. The lion was back on the prowl. I decided that an early morning run was exactly what I needed in order to get my heart pumping and my mind greased for thinking about the next great adventure for Dick Ryder.

I sat outside for a while longer, only going inside to get a second cup of coffee. The neighborhood yawned and came awake. Activity bubbled up in the houses around me and cars with men in business suits, moms with kids in the backseat growled to life and drove on by. Like the ebb and flow of the ocean, the hub of activity soon quieted down to a simmer. Now was probably the time for my summer of content. If you'll allow me to bastardize the good old bard.

There was just a tickle of fall in the air. Like the soft nuzzle of a dog's wet nose. It was ideal for a run. I figured I could run a marathon, I was feeling so energetic. But a nice and casual three to six mile jog was probably better.

I went back inside to get changed into my running gear. I love tight running shorts, but they look a bit gauche when worn by themselves, hugging the family heirlooms as if they're presented on a platter as you run forward. Turns my stomach to see men running like that. Now women, that's a different matter. So I put a pair of blue running shorts over top of my running tights. More presentable and I was still quite comfortable.

I had on a tight fitting soft blue technical running shirt, and of course my running shoes were blue, too. You probably already guessed that. I grabbed a big bottle and filled it with Powerade, two towels from the linen closet and a change of shirt, from my cupboard, for the drive back. I didn't want my Maserati's seat getting all sweaty.

One of the towels was a hand towel to drape over my driver's seat back rest and the other was a face towel for wiping my face after the run. Not that you care, I'm just telling you how I roll.

The best paths in Valley View are down along the river. Great trails both paved and natural. However, it's a ten minute drive from where I live so I got into my GranTurismo.

It was around nine thirty when I got to the parking lot of Valley Edge Park. It was half empty. It was, after all, a workday and most of the cars that were parked here either belonged to moms bringing their tots to the playground or folks who drove down here to park while they rode their bicycles the rest of the way into town.

I got out of my car and locked it up. The sky was a baby's blue with cotton swabs of white clouds. My spirit was buoyed. I hadn't thought of Janet for the last hour or so. I had taken the fork in the road. The road less traveled.

I walked over to an unruly clump of trees and did some stretching for a bit. I watched a very attractive young woman drift by on her rollerblades. She was wearing tight fitting yoga pants. Her bum was as smooth and tight as two peaches. I wanted to bite it. Maybe I'd get lucky today. I sure hoped so.

I took off running at a gentle clip, just enjoying the view and the smells of fragrant wild flowers in the air. Their blossoms were dotted over a green and yellow canvas of grassy fields on either side of the path. There were blues, pinks, reds and oranges. It was a cacophony of visual stimulus. I only saw the occasional bicyclist and runner every few minutes. I wanted it even quieter than that, so I decided to duck onto the natural trails. The unpaved paths that zigged and zagged up and down through what they call the Aspen Landing Trail.

I probably wouldn't get lucky, but that's the price you pay for enjoying some of God's unspoiled wilderness. Sex could wait. It had only been a few days since I'd last been with a woman. And that was Janet. Before that was, um, I struggled to remember their names. Ah, yes, Margaret and Sheri. Yes indeed, good times.

The path started off gradually uphill and then started to zig and zag up steps at quite an angle. I decided walking was the better part of fitness, and besides I didn't want to kill myself either. It was tough going, I was panting and my heart was racing by the time I got up to the top. It opened up to a magnificent view of the valley and across the river. I stood and stared for a moment, drinking it all in.

"Gorgeous isn't it," said a voice just to the left and behind me.

I turned around and saw a bright beaming face of beauty. She must have been in her very early twenties. Face as pale as the moon with bright blue eyes and a pixie nose. I smiled broadly at her.

"Absolutely marvelous," I said, leaning against the wooden rail with the valley dropping off behind me.

She could have pushed me off the edge and I would have died a happy man. Her face was exquisite. A porcelain beauty. I was in love, if by love I mean lust. And lusting in a big way. I reached my hand out to introduce myself. If she took it, I was about to use my secret power to seduce her.

"Hi," I said, "I'm Richard, Richard Ryder."

She took my hand. Hers was soft and slim and I thought of it curling around my hard, pulsing cock.

"Silviya," she said, "nice to meet you, Richard."

You can call me Dick, I said to her in my mind, because I'd like to give it to you.

I saw her blush, her cheeks took on a rosy glow. She looked down at my groin involuntarily. She swallowed and I heard her say in her mind, I'd like to see it first, before I decide.

Bingo, I was in like Flynn. I looked her up and down. Her yoga top was pink and sleeveless. Her bosoms were large and most likely enhanced. She had a very slim waist and her legs were covered in tight black yoga pants. I looked at her pubic mound. The Y between her legs gapped open like a small smile. I smiled back. Then I remembered I was staring so I brought my eyes back up to her face.

"Do you like what you see?" she asked.

"I like the wrapping paper," I said, "can't tell about the gift underneath, though."

She took her hand away from mine and lifted up her tank top. She wasn't wearing any bra. I had thought so, I had seen her nipples like little hills pressing against the inside of her top.

Her breasts were plastic, I prefer natural, but these were magnificent specimens of medical marvels. The lower curves were smiling at me and her breasts curved out and slightly away from her rib cage. Her areola was the size of a silver dollar and the softest smoothest pink I had seen. I wanted to suck on it, imagining strawberry milkshakes. Her nipple was a pink pencil eraser, hard and firm and perfect.

"I like it very much," I said. "You are an absolute gift of sensual delight."

Pink was my favorite color on a woman's body. The fleshy bits, the naughty bits. I always loved them just that little bit more the pinker they were. Nipples, areolas and pussy lips can be all sorts of delicious hues from the soft pink of cut strawberries to the dark chocolate brown of coffee beans. But if you put a gun to my cock and made me choose, I'd have to say the pinker the better.

"I am so freaking horny," she said to me, "I haven't been laid in over a year."

I couldn't believe it. She had no reason to lie to me, but a porcelain doll like this just had to be on every blue blooded American man's wanted list.

"I don't believe you," I said. "You are gorgeous, why would you have had such a long dry spell?"

We were facing each other and by now she had covered up her fleshy balloons, but there was no one around. I wanted her naked right now. But a part of me wanted to savor the desire, the waiting and wanting.

"Well, and I hope I don't sound conceited," she said, "but I think most men are intimidated by me."

"Could be," I said, "you would be an incredible catch."

"Anyway, how did you do what you did there, earlier?" she asked.

"How did I do what?"

"Get inside my brain and unleash my innermost drive?" she said.

"Oh that, you noticed. Not many women do. It's my secret power."

She looked at me with a raised eyebrow.

"No, really. I got hit on the head when I was young and instead of getting some sort of artistic savant-type gift I got the gift of telepathy if you want to call it that."

"So, are we going to fuck or were you just talking the talk?"

She was a forward young lady, all right. Usually I have to do a bit of leading, but this was fun.

"I thought you said you'd have to see what my dick is like first. Isn't that what you said?"

She looked down at my groin. My cock was starting to firm and unfurl like a viper.

"Yes, but you look healthy and in great shape, so I bet your cock will do too."

"Did you say cock a doodle do?" I winked at her.

She giggled and came up closer to me. She lifted my shirt and I tensed my abs.

"Ooh," she said, "that's a nice six pack you've got."

"Well, actually an eight pack if you count more carefully," I said, "but in any event, you can grate granite on these puppies."

She giggled again. She bent down and picked up a smooth round, gray stone the size of her palm. She rubbed it gently against my abs. It tickled.

"Hmm," she said. "I'm not seeing any rock shavings."

"Sorry," I said, "I'm prone to exaggeration some times. Speaking of which, would you like to see my eight inch cock?"

"Love to, but how come you guys are so set on length. Girls prefer girth to length, generally. Though I'll take 'em both if you're offering."

"Sorry, I'm not. I've only got a pencil thin eight inch wooden pole." I winked at her again.

"I'll be the judge of that."

She pulled down my running shorts, leaving my running tights wrapped tight to me like an extra skin. My cock was straining hard now to get out of its cage. It was like a truncheon pointing down my inner left thigh.

"Hmm," she said again, "I think you might not have exaggerated the size of this yummy sausage. Though it looks to me like you were way off base on the girth."

"What? You mean I'm even thinner than I ever thought."

"Oh, no," she said. "This is a thick and meaty cock. The kind I've been dying for all these long, lonely days."

I leaned back against the wooden railing. The sun beat down upon me and I cast my eyes up to the sky. It was a beautiful day. I looked down at Silviya who was squatting in front of me. To my left was a smooth boulder.

"That might be more comfortable for you," I said pointing over to the rock.

She nodded and we moved over to my left, Silviya taking a seat on the rock, her face just inches from my swollen member.

"I wonder what I should do with this prize," she said, looking at my trapped cock.

She rubbed it slowly with her right hand and then squeezed it tight. I felt hot and hard, as if all my blood had drained into my groin. I moaned.

"Oh, my God," I said to her, "I am aching for your pussy."

"My pussy will have to wait," she said. "I still want to taste your man meat."

She kept rubbing my cock up and down, slowly, rhythmically all along my shaft and over my head. It felt incredibly good. I pushed myself towards her. I felt a drop of cum leak from my head. She brought her mouth to my cock and breathed through the fabric over my head. The moist heat felt like heaven. She took her mouth and sucked on the tip of my penis through my running tights. I wanted to ejaculate right then.

"I think someone wants to cum out and play," she said looking up at me.

"He wants to cum all right," I said.

She slowly pulled my running tights down from my waist. My cock sprang free like a jack in the box. It was hard and swollen and pink and it pointed at her defiantly, its one eye unblinking. She pulled both my running tights and running shorts off me as I stepped out of them.

I thought we might get caught here. We were still on part of the public trail. Part of me wanted to get caught, the other part didn't. I just wanted this moment with Silviya to never end. Just me and her in God's kingdom.

She came up again from my ankles and as she did she stuck out her tongue and licked the very end of my hard member. She grasped me firmly with her left hand and slowly pulled her hand towards my head. A drop of clear cum bubbled like morning dew on the tip of my cock. She looked at it for a while. Then she pumped my shaft again. The bubble of clear cum grew until it was a wet tear on the end of my penis.

"Are those tears of sadness or of joy?" she asked, looking at my cum on the end of my cock.

"Tears of sadness if you let them fall. Tears of joy if you kiss them away," I said.

She smiled.

"No sad penis today," she said and she licked my cum off the tip of my cock.

"Mmm," she said, "your cum tastes delicious. Really, like vanilla pudding."

"Or candy floss?" I offered.

She looked up at me.

"Yes," she said, "you've been told this before. It makes wanting to suck your cock even more desirable."

"That is the second of my gifts," I said.

"Any others I should be aware of?" she asked.

"No, just that I have this secret power, my cock is bigger than average and my cum tastes great."

"I'll say, your cock is the biggest one I've ever seen."

She put me in her mouth as if I might melt in that hot sun and she started bobbing up and down on my shaft as I leaned into her, enjoying the wet and warmth of her pretty mouth. She looked like an angel with my cock in her mouth, sucking up and down it, as if she were made for sucking my cock.

She pulled me out of her after a while and the cool breeze felt even more cool and tantalizing on my prick. She pumped me up and down with her hand, staring intently at the end of my penis as a little more clear cum bubbled to the top. She licked it up and pumped some more and licked that up again. After a while that stopped and she went back to sucking on me. Slow and rhythmical, looking up at me every so often as I smiled at her and gave her words of encouragement.

"You are absolutely amazing," I said, "I want this moment to last for eternity."

And I meant it. Then and there, I wished I could capture it in a bubble and live it for the rest of my life.

In the trees I could hear some birds singing. Their song an encouragement as Silviya's head bobbed up and down my long shaft as she sucked me wonderfully. The fragrant smell of flowers wafted over me. I wanted to have some of Silviya. I wanted to head down a two way street.

I watched her slide her hand up and down my cock as I went in and out of her mouth. She took me out of her mouth and licked me around my head with her tongue as her hand slipped up and down my shaft on her wet saliva. I wanted to pop the champagne cork right then. But I wanted more of her.

There was an old tree just behind her that had a low branch about waist height. I took Silviya's hand and picked her up. I held her hand as we walked over to the tree and she leaned back against its trunk. I pulled off her yoga top. Her breasts beamed at me like two bright moons.

I cradled them in my hand and licked them and sucked on her nipples. They were firm and meaty in my mouth. I pinched them between my lips and she moaned. She reached down to grab my cock but I was backed away from her. I squatted down and pulled her yoga pants down along with her panties.

I helped her up onto the branch and she leaned back against the tree trunk. The branch forked off in two opposite directions and she placed a foot on each of the forked branches. Her legs were open and I gazed at her pink slit. It was wet and soft. Like a pink orchid after a light rain.

I put her folded yoga pants underneath my knees as I kneeled down to feast on her sweet pussy. She was as hairless as the day she was born. Her pussy was a tight, clean slit and I licked my tongue against her clit. She moaned and I looked up at her as she caressed each of her ample breasts in her hands and squeezed them, pulling on her nipples. I licked her clitoris and felt it firm up as I flicked my tongue over it in slow steady strokes.

I took my hands, parted her folds and dipped my tongue into her wet cave. She was sweet and salty and I dipped my tongue in and out of her again and again as she moaned and cooed.

"Fuck me, Dick," she said, "please, fuck me."

I ignored her as I drank from her sweetest well and licked her clitoris. She writhed and moaned and almost fell off the tree but caught herself just in time.

We both chuckled at it. However, the moment for making her cum with my mouth was over I decided I'd fuck her under the open canopy of sky, mottled with the netting of green leaves.

I stood up and she leaned towards me, grabbing my stiff dick. She helped guide me into her wet and soft vagina. I loved the first entrance into her. She was tight, like a glove hugging me. I pushed in slowly as she parted around me. She moaned and sighed. I pushed as deep as her pussy would let me, but I couldn't put all of me in her.

I pulled out and then pushed back in slowly. I did this a few more times as she continued to squeeze and rub her tits.

I pulled out of her again and waited. For a moment she didn't say anything.

"No," she said, "fuck me. Put your cock inside me and fuck me."

She reached for me, and as she did, I slipped back inside her and started to fuck her hard and fast. She liked that. She moaned and encouraged me.

"Yes, Dick," she moaned, "harder with your big cock, fuck me faster."

I obliged. She took her left hand and started to rub her clitoris as I hammered her with my cock like a battering ram. I saw her chest start to flush a pink triangle from her neck down towards her cleavage. I wanted to cum with her. I knew it would be soon. I felt the dam of my own orgasm rising, it was taking all of my willpower to keep it from breaking free.

"Oh my God, I'm cumming," she said.

I joined her as she moaned and shuddered. My orgasm exploded from my shaft like breaking waves on the beach. Again and again I came as she moaned and arched herself onto me.

"Oh fuck, fuck, fuck," she said as she rode her climax and orgasm all the way to its end.

I pumped her full of my inner cream. I stopped, and leaned on the branches between me. We were breathing hard. I looked into her eyes. They were a bright blue, soft and her soul seemed palpable. I kept myself inside her.

"You are incredible," I said to her after a while. After I had regained control over my breath.

"I've never had such an orgasm like that before," I said.

It wasn't exactly a lie. The best orgasm was always the orgasm I had just enjoyed.

She pulled herself up towards me as I helped her and she kissed me deeply on my lips. She pulled me off her and got down on her knees where she licked the cum off my cock and sucked me for a short while. I wanted to cum some more, but she had spent me all in one place.

We got dressed and she asked me for my phone number. I gave her my real one. She said she would call, and I hoped she would. She left down the pathway and I watched her go until she was gone like a ghost. I couldn't run anymore, my legs and thighs were tired from all the fucking. So I walked back to my car, a very happy man. A big smile on my face.

The remaining few days of the week were rather uneventful. I stayed closer to home and just minded my own business. I didn't pay much attention to Janet and she didn't seem to pay much attention to me. In reality, I never saw her over those few days, though when I was out in the front yard a couple of times I did see her Mercedes parked in her driveway. But I never saw her person. Just as well, the thought of her wasn't making me upset anymore. A calming indifference was falling over me regarding her. Just the way I liked it. If I saw her again that would be okay. If I never saw her again that would be okay too.

I ran some errands and played some squash. I thought about heading back to Valley Edge Park, thinking that I might run into Silviya again. But I didn't do that. I was satisfied with the sex we had enjoyed out in the open under God's canopy. She hadn't called me and that was okay too. If I never saw her again that would be all right. There were plenty of fish in the sea.

And as the weekend drew close the sex that Silviya and I had enjoyed started to wane. I was feeling horny again and looking for some other way to find an outlet for my sexual needs. The thing is, with the super power I've been gifted with, there are really an infinite number of ways I can have my way with millions of women.

And that was my problem. I was having difficulty choosing. I could bang the receptionist at the gym I go to. I hadn't enjoyed her naughty bits. I could always go back for a nice hot yoga session. That was a lot of fun, but I'd done that already. I was now a member of the mile high club, although those beautiful Japanese women were something special. I could easily go for seconds there.

But I was thinking of something different. Something I hadn't tried before. And there wasn't a lot I hadn't tried. A nun would be fun. Fun with a nun, I chuckled at the rhyme. But getting into a convent or other cloistered building was beyond my energy at the moment.

On Saturday morning I woke up with the biggest hard on I had had in quite some time. It was time that I got my sex groove on. As I was making a bowl of oatmeal and a pot of coffee, I had a flash of inspiration. I would seek out a mom and daughter tag team. That would be fun. I wanted something a little more risqué and spicy. The same old fucking and sucking was getting staid.

My problem was coming up with a logical place to find such a mom and daughter combination. It was something I was going to have to look into. That would be my exercise for the weekend.

I sat down after my breakfast to watch some Formula 1 racing. It was a repeat of the German Grand Prix held in Hockenheim on the twenty-second of July. It was a terrific race. I had seen highlights of it and my favorite driver, Fernando Alonso, had won. I was looking forward to watching the whole event.

By the time I had turned on the TV it was under way, but they were only on lap three. I settled down for a good afternoon of Formula 1. It was just after noon. At the first commercial break I went to the fridge and got myself a Krombacher Dark. You might think it chintzy, but whenever I'm watching a Formula 1 race I like to enjoy a beer made from the country the race is being held in. This way I enjoy a round of beers from all over the world over the course of a season of racing.

That's just how I roll. This beer is a delicious and crisp dark beer. I took off the cap and took a sip. The first sip is always the best. The first of anything is always the best isn't it?

I sat down, put my feet up on the coffee table and started watching the Formula 1 after they came back from the commercial break. The race was well under way when the doorbell rang, during lap eleven. I cursed under my breath.

I debated answering it, but then they knocked. I figured I'd just go see who it was. I took a last sip of beer and got up to answer the door.

There were two women standing in front of me. Middle aged spinsters, or so I assumed. I didn't see any wedding rings on their fingers. They wore dresses below the knee that were not very well tailored. One was in a gray dress, the other a navy blue dress. They both had on flat, sensible shoes and plain blouses that were buttoned up to their necks. They wore no makeup and their hair was in a bob. Both of them.

"Hello," I said.

I looked down at the woman in navy's hands which held a magazine. It was titled "Lighttower" and the cover was of ancient men on horseback riding next to a wall of water. The woman in gray was clutching a magazine called "Alert". The title on it was

"When will violence ever end."

"We have come to bear witness to Christ's glory," said the woman in gray who seemed just a bit older than her colleague.

I had heard of this Christ figure. A guy with a powerful suite of super powers who remained abstinent. I was both amazed and saddened by that.

"Do you know about Jesus Christ?" asked navy dress.

My loin stirred. I thought about fornication. Mothers and daughters could wait for another time. I practically had my nuns in front of me. This was an opportunity I could not give up.

"I know a little bit about him, but I'd love to learn more," I said, lying through my teeth.

I opened the door wider and invited them in. They looked at each other briefly, not quite believing their luck at a fresh potential recruit. I was licking my lips. Not quite believing my luck.

We came inside to the living room. I muted the Formula 1, and held out my hand to introduce myself.

"I'm Richard," I said as navy dress took my hand.

"I'm Rahab," she said.

I'm going to fuck your brains out, I said to her in my mind. I heard her say, ooh in her mind, replying to me.

I held out my hand to gray dress.

"I'm Aspasia," she said taking my hand in hers.

"Pleased to meet you," I said out loud, and then added in my mind, I'm going to fuck you till you cum.

She blushed and I heard her say, uh huh, in her mind.

"Please, take a seat," I said to them.

They sat down together on the couch where I had been sitting watching the Formula 1.

"Would you like a beer?" I offered. "I have some cold ones in the fridge."

"Sure," said Aspasia. Rahab nodded.

I went into the kitchen and got three more beers. I came out holding them in one hand and two glasses in the other. I had already taken their caps off so I poured Rahab and Aspasia a beer each. They took them eagerly and drank deeply from them.

"So where are you ladies from?" I asked.

"We're with Yahweh's Witnesses," said Rahab.

"And you wanted to tell me about Christ," I added.

"Um, yes, but that can wait until after you've fucked us," added Aspasia.

The amazing super power of Dick Ryder to the rescue. Aspasia had opened her legs and reached in and pulled down her prudent panties. I wanted to loosen these ladies up. See how eager they were to explore the pleasures of the flesh.

"It would really help me, if you two would start making out and licking each others pussies. That would really get me going, and I'll fuck you all day."

Rahab got up and unzipped her dress. She pulled it down. I got up and took off her blouse and her bra. Her breasts were small but I didn't mind. Aspasia got onto her knees on the floor in front of the couch and knelt before Rahab. She put her face to Rahab's pussy and started licking it. Rahab opened up her legs, turning her knees out and looked down at Aspasia.

"And behold, you will taste the fruit of the woman and you will enjoy it. And the woman will give unto you her essence," I said trying to sound like the Bible.

Rahab moaned and caressed her breasts as Aspasia knelt before her and licked her pussy.

"Sit down on the couch Rahab, and bring your knees under your arms so that Aspasia can enjoy the fleshy fruit of your loins."

Rahab sat down and tucked her knees under elbows. Her pussy gaped open, her dark black hair trimmed and clipped like a well manicured lawn. Aspasia knelt in front of her and licked her pussy hungrily.

"And you must enjoy the taste of thy womanly flesh. For it is made to be eaten and you must dine on it," I said.

After a while, before Rahab had time to cum I picked Aspasia up off the floor and undressed her. Her breasts were bigger and hung low like droopy eyes. I kissed them and sucked on them. Then I took off her dress and she stood naked in front of me.

"Sit down like Rahab and let me taste your sweet pussy," I said.

51

Both Rahab and Aspasia sat next to each other and I knelt in front of them, their pussies open and wet, covered by a soft manicured hedge of hair. I dipped my tongue into each of them. Tasting their subtle differences. I spread them open and dipped my tongue deep inside their sex caves. I opened them up with my fingers and explored their insides. I licked them and rubbed their clits with my thumbs.

They moaned and cooed and kissed each other deeply. Squeezing each other's breasts as I dined on their naked, wet flesh.

Then I got up and took off my pants and briefs. My cock was a stiff pole pointing at them. Their eyes widened at my hard, pink cock.

"You will worship my staff and my rod and you will yearn for my seed," I said.

I was having fun with my biblical transcriptions. They both got on their knees and grabbed my cock.

"Take turns," I said.

Aspasia went first, pumping my cock and sucking it as if she were trying to uncover different layers of me. Rahab watched eagerly, caressing my balls and licking them when she got the chance. After a while Aspasia gave my cock over to Rahab who rubbed it and watched it as a drop of cum crested the head of my penis. She kissed it and tasted me.

"Oh my God, you taste like heaven," she said.

"Let me taste it too," whined Aspasia.

And Rahab pumped me vigorously watching more cum leak from my tip. Then she stopped and let Aspasia lick up my cum. She cooed.

"So tasty, this magnificent cock," she said.

"You are not worshiping the cock," I said. "You must worship thy cock, your master, or be punished."

I took my cock in my own hand and slapped them on the face with it. I did this to both of them. Slapping them on each cheek with my hard cock.

"Forgive us, please," said Rahab.

"Yes, please, forgive us," said Aspasia, too.

I stopped slapping them with my hard rod. The tenderly took me in their hands and licked my shaft up and down. They kissed me all over, and sucked ever so gently on my tip. They sucked on my balls and kissed my cock all over again.

"We worship your hardness and your sweetness," they each said as they sucked on my cock and licked it and kissed it. They took me and rubbed me all over their faces.

I took Aspasia by her hair as she held my cock in her hand and I pushed my cock into her mouth. She took it eagerly. I thrust it all the way down her throat until her nose was pressed against my stomach. I held her for a while then let her go. She gasped as my cock came out of her mouth, dripping with her saliva.

I grabbed Rahab by the hair and she eagerly opened up her mouth and I thrust myself deep down her throat. She tried to gag but she couldn't. I held her face against my stomach for a long while as she tried to push away. Finally I let her go and she also gasped and breathed heavily trying to get air into her lungs.

I pushed the coffee table away.

"Get onto your hands and knees," I said to Aspasia.

She did as I told her to, but she was straight out in front of me.

"Put your head on the floor and lift your ass up to your God, the cock," I said.

She did as she was told. Rahab took my cock as I knelt behind Aspasia and she put it inside Aspasia's pussy. I thrust inside her deeply. Aspasia gasped and I fucked her hard.

"Lick her asshole," I said to Rahab and she got down to the side of Aspasia's right butt cheek and put her tongue on her brown star and started licking it. Aspasia moaned.

"Dip your tongue into her ass," I said and I watched the tip of Rahab's tongue enter Aspasia's asshole.

I fucked her hard and fast, watching Rahab lick Aspasia's ass. I took my hands and spread her butt cheeks open. Aspasia's asshole opened up just a little bit and Rahab dipped her tongue into the pink and brown hole.

I took my cock out of Aspasia's pussy and pushed it towards Rahab's face. She took it in her mouth and I fucked her in her face, deep throating her as she gagged and gasped.

I took my cock out and thrust it into Aspasia's ass. She gasped.

"Oww, oww, oww," she said and I fucked her deeper into her ass.

After a while she stopped sobbing and started to moan as the pleasure overcame the pain. I took my cock out of her ass and put it to Rahab's mouth. She opened up and I thrust myself down her throat. She gagged and gasped. I pulled myself out of her and thrust myself back deeply into Aspasia's asshole. She gasped and then was soon moaning.

I took my cock out of Aspasia's ass and put it back into her pussy. They felt different from one another. I fucked her until she came.

"What do you say?" I said to her as she started to cum.

"I worship your cock, my lord," she said.

"Good," I said and fucked her until she had finished cumming.

Then I told Rahab to get onto her knees.

"Push your face into the carpet and put your ass into the air."

She did as she was told. I grabbed Aspasia by the hair and pushed my cock into her mouth for her to polish. She sucked on it, and I pushed myself deeply down her throat. Then I let her suck me for a few minutes.

"Lick her asshole," I said to Aspasia and she did.

I took my cock and pushed it into Rahab's ass. She wasn't expecting it. She groaned and sighed and I pushed in further. Aspasia watched my cock disappear into her friend's asshole.

"Just breathe deeply and relax," said Aspasia as her friend started sobbing.

Aspasia reached underneath Rahab and started rubbing her clit as I started fucking her fast and hard in her ass. It wasn't long until she was moaning and pleading for me to fuck her more.

"Oh God, I love your cock inside me. Fuck me harder, Dick, fuck me harder."

And I obliged. I fucked her hard and fast until she came.

"Oh, how I worship your rod and your cock, master," she said to me. "I yearn for your sweet seed inside me."

I pulled my cock out of her gaping ass. Aspasia didn't need any coaxing, she put me into her mouth quickly. She sucked me long and slowly and when I pulled out of her mouth I plunged myself into Rahab's wet pussy. I slipped in easily. Aspasia started to lick Rahab's open asshole and Rahab was moaning and cooing and sighing like a steam locomotive. I watched Aspasia dip her tongue into Rahab's asshole and Rahab moaned louder.

I pulled my cock out of Rahab's pussy. I was wet and glistening with her sweet juice. Aspasia licked it all off me and hummed. I put my cock back in Rahab's asshole and she moaned in encouragement.

I was ready to pop, so I pulled out of Rahab's ass and pushed Aspasia's face against Rahab's ass. I pumped my cock, and my tip spurted a gob of cum over Rahab's ass. I pumped again, and gobs of cum ejaculated over Aspasia's face, across her eye and mouth. She wanted to put me in her mouth, she held it open but I ignored her. I came and came again, making a mess of Rahab's ass and Aspasia's face.

"Drink the wine from my vine," I said to Aspasia.

She started licking all of my warm, wet cum off Rahab's ass, moaning and cooing as she did. I came around to Rahab's face and lifted her up a bit off the floor and thrust my cock into her open mouth. She grabbed my shaft and pumped me as I came into her mouth. I felt each squirt of my warm cum hit the back of her throat and she swallowed eagerly, savoring each splash of cum I gave her.

When I was done, and Aspasia was done licking all my cum off Rahab's ass, Rahab got up onto her knees and licked my cum off Aspasia's face. Then they both kissed each other deeply, seeking out any last drops and vestiges that I might have left on them. After a while they turned to me and each took a turn kissing my cock and rubbing it over their face.

"You have been blessed," I said, "with the warmth and love of my valuable seed. Go forth and sin no more."

"Yes, master," they said.

They got dressed and left the way they had come. I managed to watch the final few laps of the race. I enjoyed taking a more authoritative role with rigid Christians.

SPECIAL DELIVERY

I watched a yellow cab pull up across the street and a beautiful woman walk into it. I was watching from my porch. The cab had pulled up onto Janet's driveway. The cabby got out of his car and helped her with her two bags. She had a medium sized suitcase and a carry on sized suitcase. Both were pink.

She looked across at me and paused for a moment. It looked like she might raise her hand and wave. But she didn't do it. She smiled, though. A small tentative smile that I did not reciprocate. I stared at her. My gaze was steady. Yeah, I was being an ass. Childish even, but I had tried giving her some friendliness some days before, when I was sitting right where I am now, on my porch. I had waved at her and she had ignored me. Besides, I was supposed to be driving her to the airport and she had obviously declined that. I mean, there was the cabby right?

She had on a very smart, navy blue suit. Her legs were in sheer stockings and she wore sensible shoes with a small heel. I saw her bend over to put something in the backseat behind the driver and her bum was wrapped taut in her navy dress. I missed not having tapped that for a while. I felt some stirrings in my loins but I ignored it. Nothing was going to happen. Sure, I could go up to her and use my super power on her to have a quickie, but I was tired and lazy.

Instead I watched her climb into the backseat of the cab. The cab reversed out and entered into the road parallel to me. The driver side was facing my porch. And there was Janet in the back seat, driver's side. She didn't look at me. She was looking into a makeup mirror and touching up her lipstick.

Her mouth was in the shape of an O and her lipstick was poking at her lips. Reminded me of how she sucked my cock before. I missed that too.

It was funny, sitting on the porch, watching Janet leave for her latest business trip and having these feelings. I had recently had some good times with a couple of Christians, that was a lot of fun. And then before that was Silviya, up in God's one hundred acre woods. She had been magnificent, but she hadn't called. I'm not going to lie, I was disappointed by that. But what can you do, maybe my super power was wearing off. Not that it should mind you.

Regardless, banging Silviya and the two Christians had helped me forget about Janet. Now she was leaving on a jet plane, don't know when she'll be back again. Forgive me, I sometimes take to bastardizing songs.

I did know when she would be back. She'd be back on the weekend. Still wouldn't want to have anything to do with me, though. But I could always make her. Summon my super power of telepathy. Or perhaps instead of sitting around and moping about it, I could get proactive instead. Find me some new pussy to fuck. There were after all, tons of fish in the sea, as they say. That gave me some renewed confidence. I'd go out and conquer. Boldly go where no man had gone before.

Though that could be challenging. I hadn't met a lot of women who were still virgins by the time I got to them. Not that I was looking for that. Still, I hadn't been with a virgin since V. And that was a very long time ago.

I watched after Janet for a while as she disappeared in that yellow cab. Didn't take long. My driveway and wall blocked the view after a short time. I sat out on the porch watching the day yawning awake. Then I went back inside to check on my business.

I run one of the most successful online sex shops, as you probably know. I was expecting some more product to be delivered. Some of the fancy gear that I had ordered on my trip to Thailand not all that long ago. I don't ship from my house, I use drop shippers, it's much easier that way. But I like to have samples of the products on hand. Not only to test for quality but to have something to try out with any lovers I might be able to get into my lion's den.

Sales had not been that good the last few months. Relatively speaking. I would still make mid eight figures in sales, so don't cry for me. Summer months are always slow. Have been for years. It's a shame really, that folks don't like to fuck around in the summer. I jest of course. Just because people aren't buying sex toys doesn't mean they aren't having sex. Though I wish they'd have more sex with more toys. Help a fella out. I'm saving up for my own private jet. Those things aren't cheap.

I josh, again. I have no interest in a private jet. Business and first class are good enough for me.

I had a few folks in the Philippines who helped me out with my business. Most of my customer support is conducted by a team in the Philippines and my web designer is out there too. Everything is managed by a local manager I pay here in Valley View. You haven't met her. Her name's Marlene Fitzgerald and she's very OCD which suits me fine when it comes to running my business.

You likely won't meet her either. I know what you're thinking, you're looking forward to me fucking her. Not gonna happen. I don't dip my pen in the company ink, even if it is the company I own. Besides, she's married with three kids. I don't do married women either. You know that. A guy's got to draw the line somewhere.

The phone rang as I was finishing up an email to my support team in the Philippines. My smartphone was on the table next to me in the study. The ringtone for now was "I'm Sexy and I Know It" by LMFAO. I'm just having fun. It's no big deal.

"Hello," I said.

"Hi," said a young female voice that I didn't quite recognize. "Is Richard there?"

She sounded tentative. Almost unsure about the number she had reached.

"This is he," I said.

"Hi, Dick," she said, her voice had warmed up considerably, "it's me, Silviya, from the bike path."

Thank you, Jesus, for small mercies.

"Hey darling, how are you doing?"

"I'm fine," she said, "sorry I didn't call sooner. I was . . . um, nervous."

"No need to be nervous," I said, "I've been thinking about you lately, hoping you'd call."

"Really?"

"For reals," I said.

She giggled.

"I was wondering if I could come over sometime and see you again. You know, maybe have some more of your big cock?"

"I'd really like that. Come on over anytime you want. Just call first to make sure I'm home."

I gave her my address and she said she'd be by within the next few days. Definitely by the weekend. My cock was hard after I got off the phone with her, but I had a big smile on my face. I salivated, thinking of her sweet, pink pussy. I thought back to that time just last week when I was fucking her brains out on the bough of the tree. I felt a trickle of cum leak from the tip of my cock.

I couldn't wait until she got here whenever that would be, during the next few days. I was going to have to get proactive. I'd said that before. Maybe I'd head back for some more yoga. That sounded like a great plan.

I checked the online studio of Valley View Hot Yoga, the place I'd had so much fun at before. They had a class starting at one p.m. There was one earlier at eleven a.m., but it was already after ten and I was still not quite up to speed this morning. I had just finished my breakfast and I needed to shower and shave.

That's what I decided to do. I wanted to be nice and fresh and clean for the ladies at Valley View Hot Yoga. Well, at least for Meadow. My bohemian little slut that she was. I took a leisurely shower, washing every crevice with scented body wash. I shaved by the sink, being careful not to knick myself. I splashed on some Van Cleef and Arples' Midnight in Paris. I'm a sucker for anything blue and this is a very nice bottle in blue with the night stars on it.

Plus it smells delicious. I'd want to eat me. This is what the eau de parfum card had to say about it: The perfectly sculpted leather-amber base of the eau de parfum celebrates precious incense and enveloping tonka bean.

WTF? I mean what exactly does that mean? But it sold me, am all about precious incense, leather whips and straps and beans. I had to look up the tonka bean. It's from a South American tree and is often used in place of vanilla. And there is a subtle vanilla undertone to the fragrance. Whatevs, it smells extremely sexy. Trust me.

I dressed myself in black slacks and a blood red shirt. I had put Mr. Johnson carefully away in red boxer briefs and put on some red socks when the doorbell rang. I wasn't expecting anyone, but my package of sex toys was well on its way. In fact it could have arrived any day now. Maybe today was the day.

I'd love to have someone to try them out with, but the delivery guys are well, usually guys, and I don't swing that way. Perhaps I'd save them for Silviya. Just thinking about her stirred my gloins. I made that word up. You've probably guessed it is a combo of groin and loins, but it means growing or glowing loins. Like my cock was already making a firm decision, if you feel me.

I walked downstairs to answer the door. I didn't peek through the peephole. One of the pleasures of living in Valley View is that we're all rich. And that usually means that crime is low. Maybe because our neighborhood watch doesn't stand for the riff raff or maybe because both private security and police patrol through here on a daily basis, oftentimes more than once a day. Whatevs, I think that's what the young kids are saying nowadays, I hardly ever look who's ringing unless I'm wondering whether to open the door or not.

So I opened the door and a young petite dark haired woman was at the door. She had driven her truck up my driveway. She had long black hair that fell past her shoulders underneath a black baseball cap. She was delicious. She was chewing bubblegum and blowing bubbles.

Her lips were ripe as tomatoes and her brown eyes were big and her lashes dark and long. When she closed her eyes she did it slowly, like she was playing with me.

"You Mr. Ryder?" she asked, looking down at her mobile terminal.

"I am," I answered.

"I've got a few packages here for you to sign for."

She handed me the mobile terminal with a stylus. I signed my name. Dick Ryder. She went off to the truck to grab the boxes and I watched her lean in through the side door and her ass beamed at me. I smiled back. Her legs were taut and brown and shapely. Her calves were strong and smooth.

She returned and put a box by the doorstep. She went back for another box and brought that to the door step. She reached out for the mobile terminal and I took a liberty.

I grabbed her hand and before she could pull it away I told her, in her mind, that I wanted to fuck her. She looked at me and giggled and said sure.

She came into my hallway without me having to ask. He breasts were ample and straining tight against her blouse.

I didn't want to piss around. I was horny as a toad and I didn't feel like schmoozing her.

"What's your name, sweetheart?" I asked.

She looked at me and blinked those big eyelashes.

"Danielle," she said.

"Take off your clothes, Danielle," I said.

She did. I watched her pull down her work shorts and she stepped out of them. She had on a lace thong that was see-through. She was as bald as the day she was born. She unbuttoned her blouse and dropped it on the floor. She wasn't wearing a bra. I guess young girls with their youth can get away with that. Her nipples were brown chocolate buttons pointing at me aggressively.

"You like what you see, Mr. Ryder?" she asked, cocking her head to one side and putting her hands on her hips.

"I do," I said, "and you can call me Dick."

"Ooh, Dick. I want to play with your dick."

"You'll get your chance," I said, "now let me help you out of your shoes."

I knelt down and undid her laces and pulled her shoes off. Then I pulled off her ankle socks. Her toes were painted pink. I looked at her panties and I could just make out her slit.

"I have some toys in here that I think you and I will have fun playing with."

She looked down at the two boxes.

"What are they?" she asked.

"I don't know, let's open them and see what Santa has brought. Follow me downstairs."

I led her downstairs into my basement where I have my sex dungeon set up. I turned on the lights and a warm, soft red glow lit up the basement. The floor was concrete. Makes it easier to clean up the spills, but it was heated and warm on the feet.

Danielle nevertheless shivered involuntarily probably suspecting to feel cold. Off to one side I had a cross that was made of smooth and stained dark wood. I had made it myself. I was very proud of it.

I put the boxes on a table and opened them up. Inside was an assortment of dildos and phalluses. There were also some leather wrist and ankle bands and bindings, some lube of assorted kinds, a cane that had a glass ball on the top, and a leather whip as well as a gag ball made of glass and attached to leather.

I took the ankle and wrist bindings and led Danielle over to my wooden cross which was in the shape of an X.

"Put your hands up against each bar," I ordered her.

She did as she was told. I placed a leather wrist band on each wrist and tied it firmly. Then I took the extra straps from each wrist and tied them through a metal loop at the top of each cross bar. Her hands were now stretched out and above her head. Her nipples were hard as stones.

I took the leather ankle bands and tied them to her ankles firmly. Then with the extra leather straps I tied them through metal loops at the bottom cross bars. I went behind her and pushed on the two cross bars, pushing them away from each other, making the X wider. Her legs dragged open. She was standing on her tippy toes and her legs made a ninety degree angle at her pussy. The same with her arms. I took a pocket knife from a drawer in the table by the wall and cut off her panties. Her pussy was an exclamation mark of sexual love.

I took a soft leather cat o' nine tails that I had hanging up on another wall and whipped her across her breasts. She moaned. The leather was soft and my wrist subtle.

I took the gag and placed it around her face and inserted the ball into her mouth. She was most compliant. I tied it tight against the back of her head. The ball was large, slightly larger than a golf ball and she strained with it in her mouth. I flogged her more around the breasts and belly and thighs. I gently rubbed the tails across her clit and pussy. She moaned and groaned and thrust herself at me.

"Have you been a bad girl, Danielle?" I asked.

She nodded her head and tried to answer.

"How bad?" I asked.

She moaned and tried to say something but I couldn't quite make it out.

"Have you been very, very bad?"

She nodded. I took the cane with the glass ball head from off the table and used some of the lube to polish it and make it slippery. It promised to enhance sexual arousal with tingling oils.

"You need to be fucked by the ball of penance," I said to her.

She nodded her head vigorously. I took the cane and smacked her on the side of the leg with the shaft. She winced. I smacked her on the other thigh and she winced some more. I took the cane by the shaft and rubbed the glass ball along her slit. She moaned and thrust her hips at me. I plunged the ball into her wet pussy and she moaned some more. I thrust it up inside her deeply and then pulled it out. I did this again and again.

I took her the gag off her mouth and let it settle down around her neck. I put the cane up to her mouth.

"How sweet is your pussy?" I asked her. "Tell me."

And she put out her tongue and I rubbed the glass ball over it. Then I pushed the glass head of the cane into her mouth. She gagged as I thrust it back against her throat. I took it out and thrust it up her love canal and she moaned. I pulled it out and put it back inside her mouth. I took it out and pushed it up her pussy again. She moaned and shivered.

"Fuck me, Dick," she pleaded. "I want a real cock inside me."

I undid her straps from the ankle and wrist bands. I brought her into the middle of the room. On the concrete floor were several metal loops.

"On your knees over there," I said and she got onto her knees. I turned her away from me. I tied her ankle straps through two loops attached to the cement floor. They were three feet apart. I pushed her face down onto the floor so she was looking off to the side. I took a silk scarf and threaded it through one loop by her neck, over and across the back of her neck to the other loop, where I tied it off. Her face was now secured to the floor. Her ass was high up in the air and her legs were spread wide apart. She was presenting herself to me.

I took her hands and tied them together at the small of her back. She was totally at my mercy.

"What are you going to do to me?" she asked with a little fear in her voice.

"I'm going to fuck you, Danielle, like the little slut you are."

I got undressed and put my clothes in a neat pile by the floor. I came over to her face and kneeled down beside her.

"This is the cock that is going to make you feel like a good little whore." I said.

I held my hard cock in front of me pointing at her mouth. She opened it and put out her tongue. I pulled my cock just out of reach. I pumped my shaft until a bubble of cum was dripping out of my tip. She pushed her tongue out further. I slowly brought my cock up towards her and she licked the cum off my cock and sighed.

"Hmm, so tasty," she said, "I want to suck it."

She opened her mouth and stuck out her tongue.

"Don't be greedy," I said, "you'll get a chance to suck on it later."

I slapped her on the cheek with my cock and I got up and walked around behind her. I knelt down on my knees and put my head towards her pussy which was wet and pink and juicy. I licked on her clit for a while and dipped my tongue into her honey pot. She moaned and writhed as best she could which wasn't much.

I got up from kneeling so low, and still on my knees I took my cock and pushed it inside of her. He pussy clenched firm around me and she sighed. I thrust deeper and she moaned. I fucked her fast and hard for a long time. I watched her head with her one cheek flat on the floor as she moaned and sighed and enjoyed the ride.

I grabbed her tied hands with my left hand and leaned back.

"Yeehaw," I said as I leaned back holding onto her bound wrists to stop me from falling backwards.

I pumped and thrust into her hard. She sobbed and moaned and I fucked harder. She shook and came. Her pussy was swollen and red and wet. I pulled out of her and her pussy stayed slightly open. I brought my cock round to her face and I placed my hands on the concrete floor on the opposite side of her mouth. I thrust my cock towards her mouth as she opened it. I thrust with my hips and fucked her in the mouth, banging up against her throat as she gagged.

I pulled out her mouth and slapped her on the cheek with my cock a few times.

"You've been a bad girl, haven't you," I said.

"Yes," she said, "I have. You must punish me."

"I'm going to," I said, "I'm going to fuck you in the ass until you cum."

"No," she said, "I've never been fucked in the ass."

I ignored her and walked around behind her. I knelt down behind her again and plunged my cock into her still warm and wet pussy. She sighed and groaned. I pulled out of her and walked over to the table and grabbed some lube. I rubbed a big dollop of lube on her asshole. She moaned some more. I rubbed lube all over my cock.

"This'll hurt a bit at first, but get over it, because I'm going to fuck you up the ass until you cum."

I slid my cock into her asshole slowly. She gasped.

"Ow, ow, ow," she said.

She took a deep breath. And then she breathed in and out quickly as if she was giving birth. I slid myself in further, slowly. Then I pulled out slowly. Her ass started to get used to it. I fucked her slowly and rhythmically at first until she started moaning. Then I started to fuck her faster and deeper. She moaned harder and louder.

"Oh, my God, Dick, I'm going to cum," she said.

"That's my girl," I said to her and with that she came as I fucked her in the ass. I pulled myself out of her ass and it stayed open. I put myself back in and then pulled out again, then back in and then out. Her ass was a pink hole of lust. She was breathing deeply.

"Oh my God, I have to have your cock. I need to taste it," she said.

I untied her from the loops in the cement floor but I didn't untie her wrists. I helped her up and she knelt in front of me. She pushed her head towards my cock and I let her have it. I took her by the hair and I fucked her in her mouth. She gagged and I let her off it. Once she had caught her breath she put her mouth back over my cock and I fucked her in the face until she was desperate for air when I let her off my cock.

"I want your cum. I want every last drop of your cum," she said.

And with that I took my cock in my hand and pumped it vigorously up and down until I ejaculated my load all over her face. With her hair I pulled her head up to face me. She opened her mouth.

"Give me all of it," she said.

And I gave her all of it. Hot steamy squirt of cum after hot steamy squirt. I painted her face with my white cum, filled her mouth, and she drank deeply from my cock. When I undid her wrist restraints she rubbed my cum off her face and licked it off her fingers until she was done. Then she put me back in her mouth and sucked me gently and eagerly, trying to be certain there was no more juice for her.

I let her go upstairs and use the shower and change. While she was doing that, I unpacked the rest of the goodies she had delivered for me. I was feeling on top of my game again. It always amazed me how good I felt after some lusty sex and a fulfilling orgasm. Though in truth, the feeling evaporated like morning dew after a day or two and I'd be back on the prowl looking for my next catch, to help stuff the growing hole in my soul.

Enough of that for now though. Now I was feeling great, and like a great Zen master, I was trying to live in the moment. Danielle came back down fresh faced and dressed in her uniform. Only this time she wasn't wearing a bra, she was also not wearing panties . Those were in my basement, no longer useful after I had cut them off.

I walked her to the front door and she asked for my number. I told her she already had it, she knew where I lived and the packing slip had that information on it. But she couldn't use it for any other purpose. I understood that, so I gave it to her again. She blew me a kiss as she left. I watched her back her truck up and out the driveway. She gave me a coy wave as she drove off.

I sighed and walked back inside the house. I had worked up an appetite and I was feeling hungry. I went back upstairs, though, to shower and change. I chose blue this time, because I wasn't feeling as horny as I had before. Blue shirts, socks, and underlings with black slacks. I didn't put on any more cologne. Even with the shower, I could still get a whiff of "precious incense" and "tonka beans".

There was this new restaurant, a vegan restaurant that had opened up in town called Veg Nation. I wanted to give it a try. On their website one of the dishes they had advertised was a maple and black pepper glazed smoked tempeh. Tempeh wasn't my favorite thing in the world. It has an unusual flavor because it is fermented soybeans, but this dish sounded tempting.

It was a little after two p.m. when I got into my GranTurismo to head out for the nosh. Veg Nation was in an up and coming part of Valley View called Old Town. It was the oldest part of the city and had recently become gentrified and much refined with upscale shops, fine dining and condominiums.

I found a parking stall right out front. I walked into the dimly lit restaurant which was full of old wooden tables and chairs and floorboards. It looked like it might have been made during the Wild West. And I say that with much admiration. It was a very inviting and warm interior. I looked around and there was only a smattering of patrons left. I counted three other tables. I guess I'd make a foursome.

A waitress with a black pageboy came up to greet me. Her skin was white and her lips were painted a cherry red. She'd play one of those very sexy vampires in a movie, and I'd let her bite my main vein.

"Welcome to Veg Nation," she said.

Her voice was smoky and raspy. She could easily be a jazz singer.

"Thank you," I said.

"Are you dining alone?" she asked.

"I am, unless you'd care to join me," I said.

She smiled and her mouth sparkled and shone a set of brilliant white teeth.

"This way."

She grabbed a menu and led me to a booth at the far end of the restaurant against the wall. She placed the menu in front of me.

"Just so you know," she said, "we close at three to prepare for dinner, but we won't rush you out of here."

I smiled.

"I'll be back in a minute to take your order."

"Thanks," I said.

I know I'd just had sex a few hours ago. Terrific, lustful sex, but I was feeling warmth again in my gloins. I wouldn't mind having her polishing my pole while I enjoyed a scrumptious meal. What the hell, I thought to myself, live a little.

I looked at the menu just to see if there was anything else on there that I might prefer. There were a ton of items I might like. Very tempting. If the service was good, I'd probably come again and again, if you'll forgive the double entendre. And, oh yes, if the food was good too.

The waitress came back smiling. She was wearing a black blouse, a short black skirt and a white apron around her waist.

"I'm Candice," she said, "do you know what you'd like to eat?"

"I do," I said offering my hand to her.

She took it.

I'll have you sucking my cock, Candy, if you don't mind, I said to her in my thoughts.

She smiled. I'd like that, I'm famished, I heard her reply in her mind.

"I meant what would you like to eat?"

Your sweet pussy, I thought.

"I'll take the glazed and smoked tempeh. How is it?"

"It's delicious," she said, "I really like the romano beans and carrots that come with it. They make a nice compliment."

"Thanks, I'll take it then, and a glass of lemonade."

"Sure thing, I'll be right back."

She trundled off, sashaying her butt as she left to put my order into the computer screen. I was looking forward to having her dine with me. Or should I say, on me.

It didn't take her long to come back out with my lemonade.

"If you'll give me a few minutes," she said, "the other tables are just finishing up and then I'm all yours."

She winked at me.

"Wonderful," I said. "I've heard great things about the service here."

"It'll blow your mind," she said.

And my loins stirred and awakened the sleeping giant. I watched her deliver the checks to the other tables. Then she disappeared into the kitchen. She came back with my meal of maple glazed tempeh. I dug into it, it was delicious. She left to help the rest of the customers finish up paying. I watched them leave. It seemed like they were taking years to go. I was getting impatient. But my lunch was keeping me busy.

Finally she locked the restaurant door with me trapped inside. She was going to make sure I paid. She came over to me and asked how the meal was.

"It's delicious," I said. "You must be starving."

"I am hungry," she said, looking down at my groin.

"Then you should have a snack," I said.

She didn't need more encouragement than that. She got down on her hands and knees and crawled in under the table. The next moment I felt her unzipping my fly and pulling my hardening cock out from my boxer briefs.

I looked down at her as she slowly pumped my penis with her hand, watching me grow hard. She licked the tip of my cock and then slowly started to suck on my head like it was a cherry flavored lollipop.

I moaned. I couldn't believe I was still this horny after the great sex I had earlier enjoyed with Danielle.

I tucked into the rest of my lunch. Piling on romano beans and carrots with bits of the tempeh. It was a delicious menagerie of different flavors. I had worked up an appetite. So had Candice. She was rhythmically sucking and pumping my cock. I was hard as stone in her mouth. I looked down at her as she worked on my penis, oblivious to the fact that I was actually attached to it. She pulled her mouth off and pumped my shaft, watching until a drop of cum crested my head. Then she licked it up greedily and sucked me more.

I was enjoying the sensation of her warm, wet mouth around me, enveloping my most private parts. I had finished my meal by now, but I didn't want to interrupt her enjoyment. It felt incredible, I imagined she might have been a professional at this, she was that good. I felt like I could melt into a puddle of warm vanilla in her mouth at any moment. But I would bide my time.

"I want to put myself inside you," I said to her.

She slid out from under the table. I got up from the booth and came over to her and took her to a table in the middle of the restaurant. I placed her on it, on her back. I reached up under her dress and pulled down her pale blue panties. I pushed up her dress to reveal her pink, shaved slit. It was wet and glistening slightly. I rubbed her clitoris with my finger and she arched her back slightly and moaned.

"Oooh," she said, biting her lower lip gently.

I pulled up a chair just in front of her and sat down on it. I put my face to her wet pussy and began licking her clit. She moaned and cooed and generally encouraged me. I licked in between the folds of her pussy lips and tasted her warm spiciness. I dipped my tongue into her honey pot and licked her clitoris. I continued to slowly and carefully lick her north and south and east and west. I explored the whole compass of her womanly bits until she shuddered, moaned and groaned in orgasm.

Then I got up and pulled down my pants and briefs. I slid my still hard cock into her wet pussy. It went in easily. Her canal hugged me. It was slippery and tight. She moaned more.

"Yes, yes, harder," she said.

And I pumped her harder and with more determination. I pushed the inside crease of her knees with my hands until her knees were close to her armpits. Her pussy was open and available. I slid in and then out. I did this again and again. She loved it. I looked up, and through the window in the door to the kitchen I saw a young blonde guy watching us.

"Come and join us," I said to him.

He looked away quickly, embarrassed to be caught.

"You're happy to service us both right?" I asked Candice.

"Uh huh," she said.

I waved him over.

"She won't bite," I said, "but she sucks really good."

He came out from the kitchen slowly and tentatively.

"Give her your cock to taste," I said.

He slowly came up to her and she reached out a hand towards him. He took off his apron and unbuttoned his pants. He zipped down his fly and dropped his drawers and underpants. His cock was firming up. Candice took it with her one hand and put it in her mouth, and sucked it gingerly. His eyes flickered and then he closed them. I fucked her harder and as I did, his cock slid into her mouth further until she was practically swallowing it.

She kept stopping and taking his cock out of her mouth so she could groan and moan and beg me to fuck her faster. I did as I was told because I'm a good boy. She put his cock back in her mouth upside down because her face was lying on the table. His balls were practically resting on her eyes. He was fully erect by this time and she was still slowly and carefully sucking him.

I felt my cum building and an orgasm growing inside me. I wanted to cum in her mouth, have her taste my sweetest essence. I pulled myself out of her.

"Time to change places," I said to him.

He drifted back to reality. Candice took him out of her mouth. I thought this young lad would probably cum at any moment. He was a young skinny guy, probably around her age with an uncircumcised penis. He went around and placed himself between her legs, avoiding eye contact with me.

I put my cock by her face and she took it into her mouth. The kitchen cook put his cock inside her pussy and started to fuck her vigorously. He was trying his best, but he was about to bust his nuts. He had no staying power, being a young buck. He was quickly in deeper than he should have been.

"Ungh," he cried as he came in her wet, wanting pussy. His show was over almost as quickly as it started.

I pulled Candice closer to me by her underarms. I did it until her head just came off the edge of the table. I cradled the back of her head with my two hands as I thrust my cock into her mouth, deeply down her throat. She didn't mind. This was a skill she had mastered. I was working up a huge load of cum again that I wanted to give to her.

I pulled myself out so that she could get more comfortable and catch her breath.

"Cum for me," she said, "I want to taste you."

That's all the encouragement I needed. I plunged my cock back into her mouth and deep down inside her throat as far as it could go. It only took three strokes and on the fourth I started to cum. I pulled my cock out slightly so that only my head was in her mouth and I pumped my shaft with my hand as wave after wave of my creamy cum erupted from my cock and filled her mouth with my tasty essence.

She swallowed, again and again, until she had drank deeply and completely from my vine. And even when I was finished she kept at me, sucking and sucking until she finally realized that I really was finished. Then she let my cock go.

"Oh God," she said, "so freaking delicious. I've never had such tasty and sweet cum."

"Thank you, Candice," I said, "that's a nice compliment.

I pulled up my pants and underwear and got myself dressed. The young kitchen cook had just left and gone back into the kitchen. Candice got herself decent. I put a Benjamin on the table by my empty plate of food.

"The meal was absolutely delicious," I said, "and the dessert was to die for."

I winked at her. She smiled.

"I hope you'll come again," she said, emphasizing the word 'come'.

"I'm pretty sure I will," I said.

And I walked out of there as she relocked the door after me. The sun was bright. The birds were singing and my knees felt weak.

GIVING THANKS

The tickle of fall could be felt in the morning air. The leaves were turning rusty. Oranges, yellows, and even reds were filling up my yard. I loved the colors. I had spent the last few days in my yard raking leaves and pulling out plants that had died or were dying. This was the circle of life I suppose. The dying so that new things could be reborn in the spring. It always gave me pause at this time of year to think about that.

And my thoughts turned to Janet and me. It had felt that at one time we were in the blooming, blossoming stage of a relationship. Lately though, it seemed like the old, shaky hand of autumn was sticking a knife into the guts of our fragile beginnings.

I knew that Janet must have been back by now. I had seen her car in the drive and then it had disappeared. It had been over a week since she left for her last business trip and I hadn't known her to be gone for longer than a week at a time. Not that I was intimately familiar with her schedule, after all, I hadn't known her that long. But I was making reasonable assumptions. Or so I thought.

I paused during my backyard chores. My yard was big enough that I was tempted to hire a yard service for this type of work. Once a year I'd think about it, during the week or so that I spent out back raking leaves, pruning bushes, and pulling dead flora out of the beds. But my yard was also small enough that I could do it myself. And I mostly liked doing it myself, except for this time of year when the repetitiveness would sometimes get the better of me.

So I stood in the yard, a small mound of dead leaves by my feet like a feathery pillow and I leaned on my rake and wiped my brow. It was still warm enough that I was perspiring slightly. And I thought about Janet.

As you can probably tell, I was having a hard time letting go of what might have been a relationship with her. I was a little confused as to the best way to proceed. I knew she wanted something exclusive and I wasn't able to give that to her. Maybe I had lost my opportunity. Maybe she had moved on. I didn't know for certain. She hadn't spoken to me since I'd dropped her off at her home after our debacle at the sex club.

And that made me wonder, too. I don't think she had enjoyed that experience much, and I hadn't either. Seeing her with a couple of other men had given me bad feelings. And I didn't like those kinds of feelings.

Yeah, you might say that I should just get over it and settle down with her. She's a catch, that's for sure, and many a man would be happy to have her as his own. But it's not that easy. My feelings are complicated; my baggage is heavy and vast. It's not just that Veronica broke my heart when I was a young and impressionable teenage boy. It's not just that I lost my parents when I was young. These things happen to others.

It's more than that. It's hard to explain. Maybe I get bored with the same woman after some time. New things are always more exciting than the tried and true. Hell, why do we keep buying new cars, computers and other stuff we don't really need, when what we already own will suffice? Because new is titillating, exciting and exploratory.

True, we could find other benefits of the old and trustworthy. They're reliable, they're certain; we know how they work etc., etc. Listen, I'm not trying to equate people with things. But there are similarities. At least for me there are.

I like to explore and enjoy new women. I like to try their pussies, the newness of their subtle bits to me. It's exciting and fun and gives me huge hard-ons. Is it shallow? Maybe, but maybe it's also the way I am. Nobody's getting hurt and I'm not doing anything my partners don't want anyway.

Okay, so I use a gift, or a super power, if you will. So I can manipulate women into wanting to fuck me and become sexually adventurous. They're not really doing anything they wouldn't want to. It's like a hypnotist. Hypnotists can't get you to do something you don't want to. My power is just able to release the inhibition that these women have, and I get off on that. The things we do together are not things they'd likely do, normally. They're hidden, deep, dark desires, if I can call it that. And that's the power. That's the thrill and the hunt and the catch.

Could I give that all up for just one woman? That's the rub. That's where I'm just not sure if I could. Like right now, I'm thinking of sex again. Am I an addict? I don't think so, maybe, but I don't care. I want sex. And I want sex with someone new. I want to explore a new wet pussy. I want to watch a woman I haven't met before put my cock in her mouth and drink my cum. This is not deviant behavior. I mean, come on, would you look a gift horse in the mouth? If you had the power and gift I have to make women your sexual slaves, free slaves mind you, would you not do it?

Show me a red blooded man who wouldn't, and I'll show you either a homosexual man, in which case he'd be using the power with other gay men, or I'll show you a eunuch.

So what is it going to be? Am I going to be able to commit or am I going to lose Janet for good? If you were going to put a wager on me, I'd suggest you bet against me committing. I don't know how long Janet can hold out. Hell, she might even now have moved on, and be in the arms of some other man who can give her monogamy.

But you know what? How many guys are out there that really, truly, can commit exclusively to one woman for the rest of their lives? I think it's less than you think. Less than half, that would be my guess. At least I'm honest. At least I'm not saying I'll commit when I know full well that I won't, and probably can't.

I'd like to be with Janet, but I don't know if I can be with her exclusively. Right now I enjoy fresh, new, pink pussy too much to give that up for her sweet pussy. Even if it is the best damn pussy this side of the Rockies. Yeah, I get lonesome sometimes. It would be nice to have someone to talk to everyday and just share life's moments with. I get it. I understand why folks get married and stick together. I can see that the journey shared is richer. But I'm still young. Maybe when I get older it'll be a different story. Maybe when I'm 65 I won't be such a horn dog, and I'll prefer the quiet comfort of one woman by my side rather than the comings and goings of several women like a revolving door.

The thing is, by the time I'm 65, Janet will probably be off somewhere else, watching her grandchildren grow up.

So, do I seize this moment with her now, while she's in my sights, or do I keep on doing what I've been doing and see if someone else will come along when I'm ready to settle down? That's a toughie. I've been with hundreds of women since V broke my heart long, long ago. And none of them have ever come close to making me feel the way I do about Janet. I was twisting myself into an enigma wrapped in a maze. I shouldn't be a philosopher; it was no good for me to philosophize. And this was one of the problems with relationships; they're too damn hard and tricky. Too many mental gymnastics involved. That was one of the big reasons I avoided them, to be honest.

So I went back to raking the yard. I was almost done. I had maybe one more, big pile of leaves to rake up and put in the bag. I got to thinking of how I could do with some more sex. Last time, you'll recall that I was looking forward to trying a tag team of mother and daughter. But I hadn't been so lucky.

Now don't get me wrong, I had been especially pleased with the little bit of S&M that Danielle and I had enjoyed after she had given me a special delivery. And boy, was it a special delivery.

And let's not forget about Candice, as sweet as candy. She was a treat, sucking my cock while I ate some delicious food at the restaurant where she served. I could have some more of her. A second helping, if you will. I made a mental note to head back to Veg Nation, her restaurant, as soon as I could. The food was good and the dessert was to cum for.

Speaking of food. It was nearly Halloween. I didn't have a lot of treats for the kids and I was noticing more and more kids visiting my home on Halloween each passing year. Either my neighbors were having more kids or there were more families moving into Valley View. Regardless, I needed to head to the store and pick up some candies for the kids.

I finished up my yard work and headed inside to shower and change. I could head out to the store looking like a bum but you never know who you might bump into and I always want to be prepared. There might just be that gorgeous woman waiting for me to introduce myself to, and I want to be presentable. Be Prepared is not just the Boy Scout's motto, it's mine too and not just because I was a boy scout once. And preparation is always a valuable motto to have at the forefront of your mind.

I changed into a pair of Earnest Sewn Hemingway blue jeans with a red t-shirt that had a blue question mark on it. My boxer briefs were red, which I don't need to tell you if you've been following along. My socks were red too, as were my sneakers. A pair of Draven sneakers. A splash of Victorinox Swiss Army Unlimited eau de toilette completed the ensemble.

Why Unlimited? Because it smells great, but also because it matched my clothes. It's in a nice rugged, red rubber case. They, being Victorinox, tell me it is "incredibly timeless and masculine with the spirit of wide open space." The guys who write the copy for colognes should be paid a mint. They make a buyer out of me, more times than not. However, I've still gotta like the scent and this one has the woodiness of silver firs matched with the aromatic spiciness of absinthe and genepi liquor. Almost makes you want to drink the stuff. Don't though. You'll probably lose your ability to have an erection.

I got into my Maserati and headed to the local supermarket. It's one of those fancy boutique stores. Not sure why I went there, there are other discount big box stores that would have worked better and saved me a ton of money. But I'm really not that concerned with money and besides, this local establishment has a much nicer environment, and it's closer too.

The parking lot was mostly empty. That's another reason I like shopping here, they don't have the same lineups as you'll find at other stores and the service is not only quicker, it's friendlier and better. That's worth paying more for, in my opinion.

I ducked in through the automatic doors and picked up a basket. One or two big boxes of chocolates and/or chips would probably be all I needed. With my sweet tooth, I didn't need to keep a lot of temptation around for me if I didn't get enough kids to come by and take the candy off my hands.

I popped down the candy and chip isle and what do you know, but there was some candy for me, too. Remember how I'd been keen on a mom and daughter tag team? Well, perhaps wishes do come true if you're a good boy. Toward the end of the isle were a young woman and a younger woman. They were together, that was for certain. They looked like mother and daughter due to similar facial features, but I couldn't be certain until I asked. And I was gonna ask because if they were blood, I was going to bang the two of them together. If the old lady wasn't married that is.

I figured the mom looked to be in her mid to late thirties and the daughter, she was probably eighteen or nineteen tops. I smiled and licked my chops like the hungry wolf I was.

I walked up to them nonchalantly.

"Shopping for Halloween?" I asked.

The mother nodded.

"What do you think the kids like best? Chocolates or chips?" I asked.

I smiled warmly, doing my best to charm them. They were still a bit icy.

"I don't know," said the mother.

Ice queen, I thought. So I looked at the daughter and asked her.

"What do you think? Should I go for candy or chips?" I asked.

She looked at me.

"Get both. Give them a chocolate and a bag of chips," she said.

I salivated looking at her full lips and pink tongue like a soft marshmallow in her mouth.

"Done," I said. "Thanks."

The daughter smiled at me. The mother barely curled her lips. This was harder than I thought it would be. I didn't see a ring on her finger, so I figured I had to be bolder than I had been to this point. I put down my basket and before they could say anything I grabbed both of their hands gently but firmly.

"Why don't you come on over to my place for some fucking and sucking?" I said in my mind to them.

The mother blushed and the daughter giggled. I heard them both say sure. Yay, for me. I picked up a box of chips and a box of mini chocolates. I gave them my address.

"We'll be right behind you," said the mother.

"I'd rather be right behind you," I said to her grinning.

The daughter giggled again, she liked that one. I paid for my Halloween candy and went to my car. She didn't lie to me, they were right behind me. In fact they stayed on my tail the whole way home. Not that I tried to ditch them. That wouldn't have been very chivalrous of me. But they kept close. I liked that.

We got home, with the ladies pulling up behind me in their Bimmer. I got out of my car and opened up the passenger door to let the daughter out. I'm old school that way. They followed me into the living room and I suggested they take a seat while I put my things away.

"How about a nice, cold, glass of wine?" I offered.

They both agreed. I went into the kitchen and fished out a bottle of white that I had in my fridge. It was an unopened bottle of Nollen Notorious Rooster Riesling 2010 in a fun blue bottle. I opened it and bought it out into the living room, carrying three wine glasses in my other hand. I poured us each a large glass of wine and gave the first one to the mother. The second I gave to the daughter and the third I kept for myself.

"Cin-cin," I said, thinking of my penis.

They both raised their glasses and we clinked.

"Cin-cin," they said.

"To my penis, then," I said.

They both blushed.

"That's what cin-cin means in Japanese," I said, grinning.

They smiled back.

"To your penis, then," said the mother.

I sat down to the side of them in my armchair.

"It was rude of me not to introduce myself," I said. "I'm Richard Ryder. But please call me Dick."

"I'm Jane," said the mother.

"And I'm Janelle," said the daughter.

"And you are related, I'm assuming?" I asked.

"Yes," said Janelle, "she's my mom."

She looked over at her mother.

"I don't believe it," I said to Jane. "You don't look anywhere near old enough to have a daughter."

Sometimes I'm a bit of a cad. But truly, she looked remarkable for having had a daughter. She was slim in her jeans and t-shirt and her face still had a youthful glow. Her brown hair was wavy and long. Her daughter looked similarly attractive and her hair was the same chestnut brown with highlights in it.

Jane smiled at me.

"You're very kind," she said. "My secret is taking care of myself."

I nodded.

"I can see that," I said.

We sipped our wine for a bit. Allowing the drink of Bacchus to oil our inhibitions.

"How old are you?" I asked Janelle.

"I was eighteen two months ago," she said.

"Have you ever had sex?" I asked.

She looked down shyly and shook her head.

"Then I'm about to ruin you for any other man you'll ever have," I said.

"That's a tall order," said Jane. "I'd like to see how you can do that."

"I'll show you," I said. "Let's head on up to the boudoir."

I got up holding my glass of wine. I offered my hand to Janelle and she took it. I led the two of them up to my bedroom. We stood in front of the bed for a moment. I didn't want it to get awkward. I rolled down the blackout screens on my windows and then closed the curtains. I lit seven candles in the room, the atmosphere was now perfect, a dim but golden hue of light that softened the skin and smoothed away any wrinkles and blemishes.

"Wow," I said, "we look even better in this light."

Jane and Janelle smiled.

"Janelle," I said, holding her by the hand. "Why don't you sit down here on the corner of the bed as I start with your mother and you can see how things are done? How I can please you, when I'm finished with your mother."

Janelle sat down on the edge of the bed. I helped Jane pull off her blouse and I undid her bra. Her breasts were ample and firm. They had been helped by modern medicine and the times of sand. I squeezed them. They were firm like well filled balloons. I knelt down on one knee and undid her denim jeans. I pulled them down to her ankles and she stepped out of them. I then pulled down her pink panties. Her pussy was a wet pink slit with a triangle of black hair like a crown just above its opening.

She stepped out of her panties and I helped her out of her socks. Her legs were shapely and firm. The gap between her thighs, where her pussy was, smiled at me. I smiled back. I stood back up and looked over at Janelle. She was looking at my groin. Jane grabbed at my crotch and started to rub my already hard cock.

I gently pushed Jane down onto the bed. She sat in front of me. Her face was at my navel. I took off my t-shirt and my abs were slabs of chocolate. Jane rubbed them gently with her nails. It felt good and ticklish. She unbuttoned my jeans and pulled on my zipper. She pulled the jeans down to my ankles and I stepped out of them. My cock was a hard cylinder under my red boxer briefs. It was pointing to my right, towards Janelle. Janelle was staring at it.

Jane pulled down my briefs and my cock sprang out like a bird from a cuckoo clock. Janelle swallowed and stared greedily at my hard dick now pointing at her mother. Jane took it in her hand and slowly started to pump my shaft up and down towards her. A drop of cum glistened from the head of my penis. Janelle swallowed and licked her lips. Her head inched forward. I turned and pointed my cock in her direction.

"Have a taste," I said.

She didn't look up at me. She opened her mouth and pushed out her tongue and she licked the top of my cock and took the drop of cum onto her tongue. She pulled her tongue back into her mouth and swallowed again. She sighed.

Then she opened her mouth and put as much of me into her as she could. She was hungry and greedy. For a woman who had never had sex, she was famished for it. I watched her bob her head up and down on my hard long shaft, gripping the base of my erect dick as if to let it go for just an instance would mean it would vanish.

She was good. Janelle sucked, and then after a while she stopped to take a break and pump my shaft with her hand, and to watch for any cum leaking out which she would quickly lick up.

Her mother was getting upset. Jane looked over at her, watching proudly at first, but then she started to get exasperated.

"Leave some for me," Jane said.

Janelle didn't hear her or, more likely, she just ignored her. After a couple more minutes of Janelle keeping all of my cock to herself, her mother butted in and tried to take my cock away from her. Janelle fought her off.

"Play nicely ladies," I said. "Janelle, let your mother have some, too. If you do, I promise I'll let you have the big surprise at the end."

That seemed to appease her and she let my cock out of her mouth and offered it to her mother. Jane didn't even say thank you, but I didn't care. She pumped my shaft like a pro. She knew exactly how to make a cock cum in bursts and spurts of fireworks. But I wasn't going to let that happen. Not yet. We were just getting started.

Jane was wringing my cock with her hands and it was making me feel extremely excited and hard. So much so, that every so often I leaked cum out the top of my dick, which she quickly sucked off with her mouth. Jane looked up at me every so often to see how well she was doing. I smiled at her and moaned to encourage her.

I was in heaven. This was a treat for me, to have a mother and daughter team.

"My turn," I said to Jane.

I gently pushed her down and upwards into the middle of the bed.

"Watch how I lick your mother's pussy, so you can do the same later," I said to Janelle.

Janelle moved in closer. I pushed the backs of Jane's knees towards her chest to expose more of her beautiful pink pussy.

"Hold your legs down there," I said to her.

Jane grabbed the backs of her knees with her hands and held them down to each side of her ample breasts. He pussy was a fleshy mound of wet pinkness that looked like a mouth I wanted to kiss. I leaned down into it and started to lick her up and down. Janelle had her face next to mine, watching my tongue caress her mother's sweet bits. Jane's pussy was flushed, swollen and wet. It smelled like forests after fresh rain.

I took my hands and spread her pussy lips open further. Her pussy gaped open more and I slipped my tongue into her and tasted her deepest parts.

She started to moan and shake. I took my tongue and licked across her clit sideways. She moaned and pulled her knees further down towards the bed. She arched and thrust her vagina towards me. She moaned and groaned, and I heard her breathing ragged and hard.

"Oh, God Dick, you're going to make me cum," Jane said.

I pulled my head away from her pussy and took Janelle's head by her hair and pushed her face into her mother's wet pussy. Janelle didn't mind, she started licking just as I had done and dipped her tongue into her mother's love tunnel.

"Oh, God Dick, I'm cumming," said Jane, as Janelle licked her mother's pussy eagerly and hungrily.

Jane came as her daughter kept on licking her, as I held her daughter's face firmly against her mother's sweet pussy. My cock was practically bursting with cum as I watched Janelle eat her mother's pussy and like it too.

I pulled my cock out for Janelle to suck on and she did. Then I put it back in Jane's pussy and started to fuck her hard and fast. She liked it that way. She moaned more quickly. So I cradled Janelle's head in my hands and lifted it up towards her mother's pussy so she could lick her mother's clit. Janelle did, and Jane went crazy with pleasure.

"My God, I'm going to cum again," she said.

I fucked her harder and faster as she moaned and begged for it. She groaned in orgasm and as she did I was ready to cum. I laid Janelle's head back down and pulled my cock almost all the way out of Jane's pussy, leaving the head of my penis in her wet tunnel. I took my hand and pumped my shaft and wave of explosive wave of orgasm came over me and I ejaculated into her deep, wet canal.

Spurt after spurt of hot, steaming, creamy cum erupted from the end of my hard cock and I filled the inside of her pussy till she was almost bursting.

When I was finished I slid out and came around the bed to the other side where Jane leaned up towards me, and took my glistening wet cock in her mouth and I ejaculated more gooey cum for her to enjoy. I could see Janelle eating my cum out of her mother's pussy as Jane kneeled into a more upright position and my cum seeped out of her tunnel.

And then we were done. I let them shower and change and I saw them out the front door. They climbed into Jane's BMW and they both gave me a shy wave as Jane backed out of the driveway. They were gone down the road quickly and I walked back into the house and sat down in the living room. I was tired and satisfied. I got up and walked into the kitchen to make myself a peanut butter and jam sandwich. I washed it down with a glass of juice. The rest of the day was quiet and uneventful.

The next day was Wednesday. It was Halloween. I had the candy ready in a bowl for the kids. I had the chips in another bowl. The afternoon dragged along slowly. I was sitting on the couch watching the TV. News came on at five p.m. I don't usually like watching the news; it's so damn depressing, usually. And tonight was no different. Someone had done somebody something bad. I was passing time. Waiting for the kids to come and eat my candy.

It was five-fifteen when I heard the doorbell chime. I looked at the TV to check. They had the time on the top right corner of the news desk. This was early for the kids to be coming round for candy. I didn't recall the first of them coming much before six p.m. At least if memory served me right. You'd think parents would want to have given their kids dinner before sending them out to collect candy. At least that's what I would do if I had kids. But if the kids were coming calling for candy, then candy it would be that I'd give them. So I got up to answer the door.

For a moment I couldn't quite believe my eyes.

"Hello," I said to her.

"Hi," she said looking down. In her hands was a bottle of wine.

"Hello," I said again. It was Janet.

I was a little dumbfounded. I had given up on her. But yet, here she was, standing right in front of me looking as beautiful as the first day I had seen her. We stood for several seconds looking at each other.

"May I come in?" she asked.

I nodded and I cleared my throat.

"Ah yes, please, come in," I said.

I moved aside and she stepped into the hallway. I closed the door after her.

"You look marvelous," I said.

And she did. She had on blue slacks and a pale yellow blouse. Her hair fell naturally down by the side of her face and across her shoulders.

"Thank you," she said. "You don't look too bad, yourself."

I smiled. She offered me the bottle of wine. I looked at the label, it was cream colored. It was a Nicolas Catena Zapata 2008. A very well liked wine; and an expensive one too. I was certain she had paid over one hundred dollars for it. I was impressed.

"Lovely choice," I said cradling the bottle in front of me like a fragile baby.

More awkward silence.

"Um, come on in, let's open this bottle and have some."

This was the best I could come up with. I led her into the living room, turned off the TV and put on some music. I didn't know what I had in the CD player. I was pleasantly surprised to hear Kenny G's "Breathless". Easy listening, romantic melodies. I saw a smile crease Janet's cheeks.

I went into the kitchen to pour us each a glass of wine. I took a sniff and a mouthful. It was yummy. Creamy and smooth. I came back into the living room and offered her a glass. She took it. I held mine up to hers.

"To us," I said. "On Halloween."

That was the best I could come up with on such short notice. I was still taken aback that Janet was here, in my home again. It had to have been a couple of weeks at least. I had no idea why she was here. She clinked my glass with hers.

"Salut," she said.

"No cin-cin?" I asked cheekily.

She laughed, and shook her head. We sat in silence for a while listening to Kenny G. I was in my recliner and she was on the couch.

"Don't get me wrong," I said, "I'm delighted to see you, I'm just wondering why you've come over?"

She looked into her glass of wine for a moment and swirled it around slowly. Then she looked up at me shyly.

"I missed you," she said.

"I missed you, too," I answered.

And then the doorbell rang.

"Kids," I said. "I think the mad rush on the Ryder chocolate factory is starting."

I got up to answer the door and Janet got up with me. I opened it to see a ghost and a pumpkin. They were probably no older than six and eight. A brother and sister.

"Oooh," I said, "very scary."

And I handed them a chocolate bar and a bag of chips. They had me dump it into their pillow cases. These were huge pillow cases. Must have been King size, I was pretty sure. Mom was standing back several feet. I waved at her.

"They're optimistic," I said, pointing at their pillow cases, still quite empty of candy, but the night was young.

"It's a good neighborhood," she said back.

And it was. Especially now that Janet was back. It felt like home. It felt natural and how it should be. The two of us in my house together, handing out Halloween candy. Like an old married couple. And maybe I'm being a little sentimental, but I sorta liked it. At that moment I wasn't thinking of any other women. Just Janet. And the future looked kinda good with her in it.

For the next almost four hours we answered the door and handed out candy. We were a great team. We must have received almost fifty kids. I stopped counting after three dozen. We almost ran out of candy and chips. But then the tide of ghouls and goblins died down, and by nine p.m. I blew out the candle in the jack-o'-lantern and turned off the outside lights.

"Are you staying over?" I asked when we retired to the kitchen to clean up.

"If you want me to," she said.

"I want you too," I answered.

I finished washing up the glasses and put away the rest of the candy. I went up to her and hugged her tightly.

"I missed you," I said to her. "I'm so glad you came."

She hugged me back.

"Let's go to bed," she said.

And she led me upstairs to my bedroom. We took off each other's clothes after I had lit several candles. Her body was warm and golden in the light of the flickering flames. My cock was erect and hard. And I wanted only her. She was all I wanted, all I had ever wanted, at that moment.

I lay her down on the bed and she spread her legs open to me, and I entered her slowly and methodically. I made love to her as she lay underneath me. I kissed her nipples and the curves of her breasts. I kissed her on the forehead and deeply on her sweet, wine flavored lips. And we looked at each other, our eyes locked together as we made love as one. We searched the depths of each other's souls and liked what we found.

And when I came, she came with me and a tear rolled out of the corner of her eye. I finally took myself out of her and lay on top of the blankets with her at my side. I was spent, but I had never felt so content and full after having had sex. It was almost a new experience for me.

I propped myself up on my left forearm and brushed her hair behind her ear.

"Why the tear?" I asked.

She looked at me furtively and then she looked up at the ceiling.

"Because I feel so good when I'm with you, dammit."

"Then why the tear?" I asked again.

This time she turned towards me and looked at me.

"Because I want you. But I want you to myself and I don't know if I'll ever be okay with sharing you."

And she burst into tears. I got up and went into the en suite, I came back with a box of tissues and I offered her one. She dabbed at her tears and she blew her nose. She didn't look at me. I took her chin in my thumb and forefinger and lifted her face towards me. I kissed her on the mouth, and our tongues darted and touched cautiously, carefully. Then I looked at her.

"I'm willing to try," I said.

"Try what?" she asked.

"I'm willing to give you and me a try. Just the two of us," I said.

She smiled and then she shook her head.

"I don't want you to do anything that you don't want to do."

She looked down at the bedspread.

"I want to," I said.

Then she came to me and kissed me passionately again. And when she pulled away more tears were streaming from her eyes.

"Oh, Dick," she said, "I love you so much."

And there was a lump in my throat. And it didn't hurt too badly. My heart felt soft and squishy and it ached. But it was a pleasant ache. What the hell, I thought to myself.

"I love you too, Janet... dammit," I said.

She smiled and for once in the longest time, life again felt full, and whole and complete.

ABOUT CANDY NYTES

I love reading romance and erotica especially. I also write mostly erotica as you can tell. I enjoy quiet evenings at home with my partner watching movies and eating extra buttery popcorn.

When I'm not reading or writing I knit. Mostly I knit dog sweaters, and human scarves and sweaters and I give them as gifts to family and friends. I live with my boyfriend and two Bichon Frise bitches.

Sometimes when I'm thinking of different romantic scenes for my books we try them out to see how much fun they are first ;)

If you'd like to get a hold of me you can reach me at candynytes@gmail.com. Pop on over to my website for up to date info on the continued Dick Ryder saga: www.CandyNytes.com

OTHER BOOKS BY CANDY NYTES

The four books you've just read in "The Adventures of Dick Ryder" series are stories numbered 5, 6, 7 and 8.

Below is a complete list of the stories in order:

1.   Neighborhood Watch
2.   House Call
3.   Mile High
4.   Hot Yoga
5.   Swing Time
6.   God's Witnesses
7.   Special Delivery
8.   Giving Thanks

The first four stories numbered 1, 2, 3 and 4 are also available if you want to own the complete collection of "The Adventures of Dick Ryder" series. Below is the Four Pack which has the first four stories included:

1.   The Adventures of Dick Ryder: Four Play Volume 1

Please visit me at www.CandyNytes.com for all the places where my erotica fiction is available for purchase. My stories are available on all e-readers and the collections are available as paper as well.